BABY LOVE

The Angeline Gower Trilogy

Louisa Young

THE BOROUGH PRESS

The Borough Press
An imprint of HarperCollins*Publishers*
1 London Bridge Street
London
SE1 9GF

www.harpercollins.co.uk

This paperback edition 2015
1

First published by Flamingo, an imprint of HarperCollins*Publishers* 1997

A catalogue record for this book
is available from the British Library

ISBN: 978-0-00-757798-9

Set in Perpetua by Palimpsest Book Production Ltd, Falkirk, Stirlingshire

Printed and bound in Great Britain

MIX
Paper from
responsible sources
FSC™ C007454

FSC™ is a non-profit international organisation established to promote the responsible management of the world's forests. Products carrying the FSC label are independently certified to assure consumers that they come from forests that are managed to meet the social, economic and ecological needs of present and future generations, and other controlled sources.

Find out more about HarperCollins and the environment at
www.harpercollins.co.uk/green

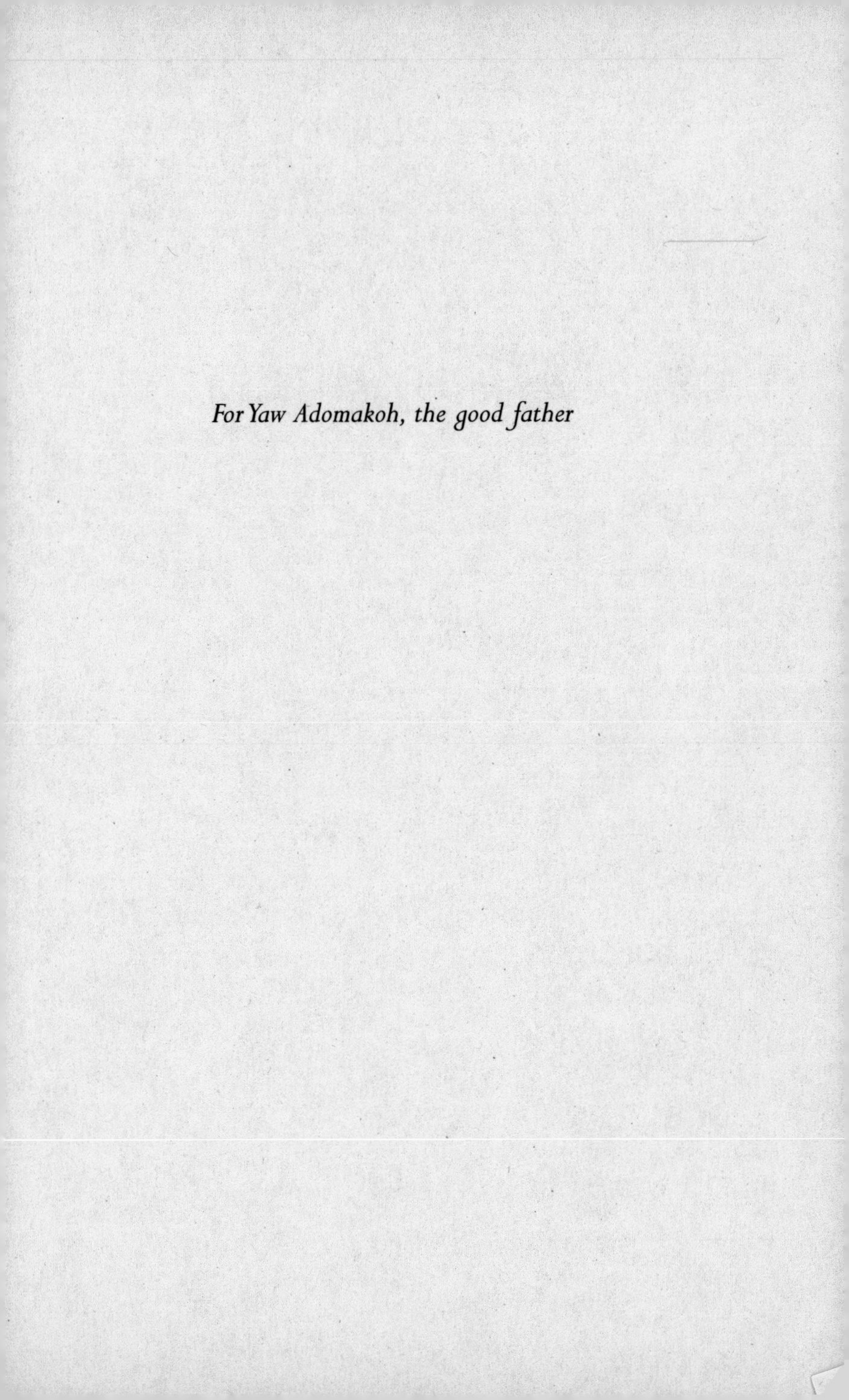

For Yaw Adomakoh, the good father

Introduction

I wrote these novels a long time ago. I spent my days correcting the grammar at the *Sunday Times*, and my nights writing. I could no longer travel the world doing features about born-again Christian bike gangs in New Jersey, or women salt-miners in Gujarat, or the Mr and Mrs Perfect Couple of America Pageant in Galveston, Texas, which was the sort of thing I had been doing up until then. I had to stay still. I had a baby. Babies focus the mind admirably: any speck of time free has to be made the most of.

I had £300 saved up, so I put the baby and the manuscript in the back of a small car and drove to Italy, where we lived in some rooms attached to a tiny church in a village which was largely abandoned, other than for some horses and some aristocrats. A nice girl groom took the baby to the sea each day in my car while I stared at the pages thinking: 'If I don't demonstrate some belief in this whole notion of novels, and me as a novelist, then why should anyone else?'

Re-reading these books now, I think, 'Christ! Such energy!' I was so young – so full of beans. I described the plot to my father, who wrote novels and was briefly, in his day, the new Virginia Woolf. After about five minutes he said, 'Yes, that all sounds good' – and I said, 'Dad, that's just chapter one'.

It was only about twenty years ago, and a different world. Answerphones not mobiles, no internet. Tickets and conductors on the bus. And it was before 9/11, and the mass collapse of international innocence which 9/11 and George Bush's reaction to it dragged in their miserable, brutalising wake. Could I write a story now, where an English girl and her Egyptian lover meet at the surface of the water? Yes, of course – but it could not be this story.

Anyway, I have grown up too thoughtful to write like this now. I exhaust myself even reading it.

I see too that these, my first novels, were the first pressing of thoughts and obsessions which have cropped up again and again in things I've written since. It seems I only really care about love and death and surgery and history and motorbikes and music and damage and babies, and the man I was in love with most of my life, who has appeared in various guises in every book I have ever written. I realise I continue to plagiarise myself all the time, emotionally and subject-wise. And I see the roots of other patterns – *Baby Love*, my first novel, turned into a trilogy all of its own accord. Since then, I've written another two novels that accidentally turned into trilogies – and one of those trilogies is showing signs of becoming a quartet.

People ask, oh, are they autobiographical? I do see, in these pages, my old friends when we were younger, their jokes and habits, places I used to live, lives I used to live. I glimpse, with a slight shock, garments I owned, a bed, a phrase . . . To be honest I made myself cry once or twice.

But, though much is undigested and autobiographical, in the way of a young person's writing, I can say this: be careful what you write. When I started these novels I was not a single mother, I didn't live in Shepherds Bush, I didn't have a bad leg and I wasn't going out with a policeman. By the time they were finished, all these things had come about. However as god is my witness to this day I never have never belly danced, nor hit anyone over the head with a poker.

Louisa Young
London 2015

ONE

An Argument

I had had one hell of an evening one way or another. I didn't want to see the guy in the first place, but when you've known someone twelve years it's never quite the right time to tell them to go away, specially when you owe them, and I owed him. Well, let that be a lesson to me.

Neil likes me more than I like him. Neil used to ring up and say, 'When can I see you? Tonight tomorrow Wednesday Thursday Friday Saturday Sunday or any day next week? Or the week after?' I liked Neil too – still do – he's funny and kind, a clever lawyer, probably too good for me anyway. But I'm not the kind of woman who gets a kick out of a good man trailing his unrequited love around in front of her like Raleigh's muddy cloak. So I tell him, and then he starts saying, 'No, look, it's fine, really, it's not the same as it was, look, I can accept it. Really.'

And I say OK, because I'm not so vain as to believe a

man's in love with me when he's saying he's not any more. And then two weeks later something comes up and there is occasion to say, 'But you said you weren't in love with me any more!' and he turns and says, 'Don't ever believe me if I say that.'

So that was Wednesday evening. My friend Brigid, who is a star, and the sort of woman I'd really like to be if things – including me – were different, came round to babysit and I thought Neil and I might go to the pictures. That way we could avoid being pissed off at each other over a dinner table all evening. He wasn't having it. He'd booked a table. He was going to insist on paying, too, and he was going to get his money's worth of making me feel bad because he felt bad because I didn't like him as much as he liked me.

So we ended up in one of those unpleasantly modern Italian restaurants in Soho, in which plate glass and cackling pretentious drunkards have replaced all the perfectly nice straw-wrapped Chianti bottles and Sicilian donkeys hanging from the ceilings which used to be there in the old days. I picked at my over-cooked tagliatelle and drank too much over-priced Soave, and he bitched at me.

Neil doesn't drink. I do. We'd fallen into this habit over the years where after a night out he'd drive me home in my car – or on my bike in the old days – and then get a minicab from round the corner. He never asked to come in except sometimes in the old days when we were young and skint, when he'd sleep on the sofa and I'd resent his presence the next morning. He never tried to kiss me. It was a great relationship.

Anyway that night I lost my temper with him. We were at a red light on Shaftesbury Avenue and he said, 'So are you free next week?' It's a ridiculous question. He knows I stay home with my kid anyway, but what gets me is that if I did spend all my time in nightclubs dancing the lambada with a camellia behind each ear and a handsome Argentinian in my arms it would be none of his damn business. And I said, 'Neil, don't interrogate me.'

He looked at me, and then he did something that he loves to do – he walked out. This is normally nothing more than irritating (or a relief) but at a red light just by Piccadilly Circus on a Friday night at closing time it was actively inconvenient. He stepped out of the car, slammed the door and walked off into the crowd.

'For fuck sake!' I yelled, and the lights changed, and the cars behind started honking. So I slid into the driver's seat and took off.

I turned into the first side street I could. Rupert Street. Unfortunately it was one way. The other way. The policeman hanging around on the corner couldn't believe his luck. I couldn't believe mine either.

*

Getting done for drunken driving and driving the wrong way up a one-way street is not necessarily the end of the world but it was near as dammit for me.

After all the ritual humiliation – it really is a drag not being in the right – they let me out of the station at about three in the morning, but they wouldn't give me my car keys. I made them unlock the car for me to take out a bottle of vodka I had on the back seat. It just confirmed their suspicions. I found a taxi – I think the driver knew what time they let the drunk drivers out and made it a regular pick-up point – and got home. They hadn't let me ring home either so Brigid was lying in half-hysterical half-sleep on the sofa when I let myself in. I looked in on Lily. She was deep in the sleep of the ignorant, golden-pink and fragrant. I could hear her tiny breathing.

Brigid's a lovely woman but she can shriek when she has a mind to.

'Where've you *been*?' she shrieked. Well, it was a fair question. I'd told her not a minute after midnight. Brigid is the nearest thing I've had in a long time to parents wanting me home on time. She has pale red hair and four children and every human quality except beauty. How does a woman with four children come to be babysitting? By a precious combination of every human quality and a gaggle of sisters, all in the neighbourhood, who fight among themselves for the privilege of babysitting their nephews and nieces, thus liberating Brigid to sit for me. It's an unspoken thing among them. Brigid needs money, I need time, women need to help each other. It works. Brigid's been babysitting for me and worrying about me ever since I got Lily, and I like her. Actually she's a friend. And so are Maireadh and Siobhan and Eileen and Aisling.

'Don't shriek,' I said. 'Just don't shriek or I'll cry.'

'Don't cry!' she shrieked. I looked at her and she must have understood my look because she went to the fridge.

'I've got it here,' I said, opening the bottle of vodka.

'I was looking for the milk,' she said. 'I was going to make you a cup of tea.' She got me a glass and an ice-cube anyway. 'What happened?' she said.

'I've been in gaol,' I said. She knew that was a joke so she laughed. Even as I let her laugh the repercussions were running through my brain. My threat to cry may prove not idle yet, I thought. But I don't cry. And I didn't need to cry, I needed to think.

Brigid was still saying, 'So what happened?' I told her, briefly. I didn't think she'd pick up the ramifications and she didn't. I told her to go home. 'It's all right,' she said. 'Maireadh's there with the boys. She's been arguing with Reuben so she's staying.'

'Where's Eileen then?'

'Still there. Maireadh's on the settee . . . I'll sit with you a while.'

It was an honourable thought, so I let her for five minutes or so, then I made her go.

I poured the vodka and stared out the window at the stripy petunias in the hanging basket across the way, glowing in the midsummer midnight half dark. Only about half the bulbs in the streetlamps on my estate are ever working at one time, but in summer along the dim dirty red-brick walkways there is always the gleam of petunias in a hanging basket.

*

My baby isn't mine. It sounds strange to say it, because she is so much mine it hurts, but technically she's not mine. My sister Janie was killed three years ago in the same crash that screwed up my leg. She was on the back of my bike. I was riding it. I was not responsible. Like hell. Technically, I was not responsible.

Lily was born just as Janie died, snatched from her belly and the jaws of death. It must be weird doing a Caesarean on a dying woman. I wasn't there. But as soon as I was conscious I knew.

The baby was in intensive care. Janie was in the morgue. My mother was in despair. My father was incandescent with rage. I was in traction. And where was Jim, Janie's about to be ex-boyfriend, or so she swore though she never got round to telling him, or he never got round to listening. We didn't know where Jim was.

'You mustn't worry about it,' my mother repeated like a mantra over the hospital soup. 'You just take time to get better. You mustn't worry. You mustn't worry.'

She was talking to herself, of course, telling herself not to worry. Just chanting, quietly, for comfort. She was in shock, I suppose. Dad just strode the green-tiled corridors, up to the baby unit, down to me, up to the baby unit, down to me. He was like one of those depressed animals in the zoo, repeating and repeating his movements, up and down, up and down, to and fro, to and fro, in the cage of his disbelief. I was no different: my thoughts spun to and fro like her words and his feet. 'Where's Jim, how can we keep the baby from him, when can I walk, when can I walk, where's Jim, I've got to get the baby, when is Jim going to walk in here, when can I walk, where's the baby?' You never know how grief will get you, until it does. All I wanted was to do things, as if doing things might change the big thing. But I couldn't do anything. Not even the normal things you do whether or not there is grief. Couldn't go out, or be at home, or cook, or move . . . I filled my time by demanding to see doctors, as if the more I saw of them the quicker I could be better. All that happened was they began to hate me.

There was a nice nurse, Dolores. She was on nights, and didn't make me take my pain-killers. 'I have to think,' I said. 'Don't make me drugged.'

She went along with me for a while and then said: 'You're only thinking the same things over and over, why bother? If you're not going to do anything, you should just get some proper rest.'

'How do you know what I'm thinking?' I asked her.

'You're talking in your sleep,' she said.

I told her about it. How Janie was only on the back of my motorcycle eight and a half months pregnant because

Jim had made one of his fairly regular phone calls that he didn't give a fuck about any fucking injunction she said she'd take out and he was coming over now. How he'd done it before. How Janie preferred a dashing escape courtesy of her sister. How I didn't know for certain that what she escaped from would have been as bad as what she got.

What if Jim comes for Lily?

'What if he comes!' I was shouting, shouting and fighting through flame, floating, clutching a child, someone was holding my ankles and my leg came off in their hand, and I floated on up and up without it . . .

I woke to find myself in Dolores' arms, my head on her shoulder. The nightlights glowed, the plumbing rumbled. Hospital smell, hospital heat. Dolores' big brown eyes in the dimness. Why am I so comforted by the idea of an African night? She gave me a glass of water and wrapped a blanket round my shoulders.

'I looked upstairs before I came in,' she said. 'The little one's OK. She's weak but she's OK. No one going to take her anywhere, that's for sure.'

'He's her father,' I mumbled.

'She registered yet?'

'No.'

'Nobody knows who's her father then. We don't know him. Her mother dead.'

'He's a pig.'

'You can't do anything yet,' she said.

'He could turn up any time.'

'Child's on a tube. She's not travelling.'

'I must have her. I must, you know.' I knew. There was never any question. Little Janie, my little sister, all of ten months younger than me.

'Think about that then,' said Dolores.

'Yes.'

'Can you keep her? Can you feed her? You a sensible woman? What your husband say?'

'No husband.'

'That's hard.' I looked up at her. She knew how hard it was.

'How many do you have?' I asked.

'Three,' she said. 'Kwame, Kofi and Nana. My mother helps.'

I can keep a child. I can work. (Jesus. I'm a dancer. My leg is in traction. I'll have to be something else, then. Can I work? Yes. There is no question.)

'But he'll be able to take her.'

'Fight for her.'

Fight. How? In court? Adoption? How does that work? He'd have to agree. Would he agree? Would he have to agree?

'I tell you two things,' murmured Dolores. 'Possession is nine-tenths of the law. And nothing succeed like a *fait accompli*.'

'When can I walk?'

'Consultant coming round in the morning.'

He won't tell me anything. They never say anything in case you sue them when it takes longer, or doesn't work out the way they said it might. Got to walk, got to walk.

I slept again, and dreamt of *faits accomplis.*

*

The next morning I had the day nurse wheel the ward pay-phone over to me and called Neil.

'Janie's dead and I want to keep her child.'

Neil was silent for a moment.

'Janie's dead.'

'Yes.'

He started crying. I sat there. Fed in another 10p. I didn't cry. He continued.

'I'm so, so . . .'

'Yes,' I said.

'How?' he said.

'Crash.'

'But the baby . . . ?'

'Fine. Early, but fine.'

'And Jim?'

'Neil, we haven't seen him. I don't know if he knows. But Neil – you mustn't tell him. They had a row . . . Look, come and see me. Please.'

'Yes, yes . . . of course.'

'I'm in hospital.'

'Oh, God – are you all right?'

I burst out laughing. Then crying. 'Come this afternoon. This morning. Come now.'

When he came he said the only thing to do was to get the baby out of hospital as soon as it was safe to do so, take her home, and hold tight. Apply for parental responsibility. If Jim showed an interest, fight it out. 'Get her home and love her and be a good parent,' he said. 'Any judge will respect that. And get married.'

*

You see why I find it hard to be mean to Neil. The petunias gleamed at me like clear thoughts in a mist of confusion. It's been three years and for those three years Jim has not turned up. I kept track of him. He is well off and well respected, and his nature remains better known to me than to the police or to anyone with any influence over the situation. It's up to me to make sure he never sees Lily again.

Therefore I don't need anything on my record. Anything at all. I could make a living without the car, that's not the problem. The licence itself hardly matters. What matters is the good name. I need my good name to keep her.

I'd been balancing it up. Seventeen unreported black eyes that he gave her (I kept count) and one injunction that she never brought versus several thousand quids' – worth of lawyers saying that I'm a drunkard, irresponsible, incapable, single and not the child's parent. That's what I was thinking about. That and the fact that that morning, the morning of the night I was out with Neil, Jim had rung up and left a message saying he wanted to talk to me.

*

I slept a little because you have to. At around seven I came out of a bleak doze to find that my mind was made up. An hour later I got on the telephone to a certain police station. I didn't think Ben Cooper would be there but it was possible and I felt I should move as quickly as I could. I was in luck, I suppose. He was there.

Ben Cooper. We first met when we were both instructors on a motorbike road safety course – he as a young cop, me in one of many attempts to prove myself normal, fit, helpful, a credit to the community and in steady employment. Ben Cooper the Bent Copper.

'Hello, stranger,' he said when he came on the line. He always said that. It was his little joke. In fact we saw each other occasionally. Not by design, but just because he made a point of never letting anyone go, just in case. I'd been trying to let go of him because I don't like the guy, and in fact I don't think I'd seen him to talk to since Janie died.

I didn't want to ask him, but I honestly thought it was the right thing to do. Perhaps my thinking was screwed. Perhaps the cold light of dawn that you see things clearly by is meant to come with sobriety after a good night's sleep, not still half-drunk after a night of fretting. Whatever.

'Ben,' I said. 'Can we meet?'

'Mmm,' he said.

'Slight problem,' I said.

'Want to cry on my shoulder?' he said.

'Mmm,' I said.

'Professional shoulder?' he said.

'Mmm,' I said.

'Anything you want to tell me now?' he said.

'Can I?' I said.

'I'll call you right back,' he said.

Two minutes later he had the gist. He took the arresting officer's number and my registration number and the case number and a load of other numbers and I took the number 500, which was how many quid his professional advice cost these days. Cheap at the price if he could do it.

'Oh, I can do it,' he said. 'You get some sleep. You sound terrible.' I didn't tell him Lily was due at nursery in an hour and a half.

TWO

In the Pub with Ben

I took Lily into nursery on the bus. It seemed years since I'd been on one. It smelt the same; grimy London Transport smell, like coins. The day was getting ready to be warm. The clippie gave Lily the dog-end of the ticket roll and told her it was toilet paper for her dolly. Lily went bug-eyed with delight and the clippie crooned at her. I was impressed. A nice old-fashioned bit of London-ness on the Uxbridge Road.

I left Lily with the hamsters and wax crayons and went up west to fetch the car (yes I know the West End is east of west London but the West End is Up West, it has to be). My blood alcohol level was probably not much lower than it had been when they pulled me, but no one was counting at nine in the morning. I drove back to Shepherd's Bush and slept for two hours.

The phone woke me. Usually I'd just roll over and let the machine take it but I was nervous and so I found that I had answered it before I was even awake. It was Jim.

'I want to see my daughter,' he said.

'Fuck off,' I said.

'Angie, listen,' he said. Arrgghhh! Don't want to listen won't listen why should I listen?

He went into a speech. He must have prepared it carefully but its niceties were wasted on me, drowned in hangover, sleeplessness and anger. I could hardly hear his voice for the NO NO NO ringing in my head.

Then I woke up. Woke up too to the fact that he was being reasonable and I wasn't; he was being civil and I wasn't; that everything from here on in can be taken and used in evidence.

'Hello?' I said. 'Hello? Who is that?'

'Angie? It's Jim.'

'Jim! God – hello. Oh . . .' I tried to convey double confusion: natural confusion at it being him, and further confusion to give the impression that I had thought that it wasn't him.

'Jim, I'm sorry, you woke me up . . .' Shite, should I admit that? Bad mother sleeps late in morning, answers phone when incompetent, what if it had been an emergency call from the school?

'What? Er . . . did you hear what I was saying?'

'No. I mean. Jim – why are you calling? What do you want?'

He relaunched. He sounded nervous – not surprisingly – and somehow well-intentioned. He was breathing as if he was reminding himself to.

'Angie. Um. I know it's been a long time and I know this is going to come as a shock to you but as you know I never intended that my separation from my daughter should be permanent and the time has now come when I think it would be the right thing for . . . for us to meet. I want to meet her. To see her. Meet her . . .' His voice fizzled out. He's as nervous as me, I thought. He really wants this.

Fear took my heart in both its hands and squeezed.

'I don't think I can say anything about this until I've had some advice,' I said finally.

'Please don't make things difficult,' he said quickly.

'Things are difficult,' I said. 'Um. Thank you for telling me what you want, it's registered, I'm going to have to think about it. You understand I can't just say "Yes of course" or "No way". I have to think about this. I'll try and think how it can be done. If it can be done. You must think too. This is a big upset, Jim . . .'

'I only want to see her, for God's sake . . .'

Immediately I knew that that was not all he wanted. This was a first step. This was a softening up. I don't know how I knew. Because I knew him, I suppose, and knew the way he would apply first sweetly and charmingly and then the moment he was crossed in the tiniest things he would become petulant, stamp his tiny feet, sulk. Then hit out. His nerves did not make him any the less dangerous.

'I'll ring in the next few days, Jim,' I said, making it cordial. 'I have to speak to some people. I'm not saying it's not possible—'

'That's not actually for you to say, you know.'

'I'm not saying it, Jim. Just that it needs some thought. You think too. Think on this, for example: she doesn't know that you are her father. She has only just realized that other children have fathers, and she hasn't yet registered that she might have one . . .'

'All the more reason,' he said.

'Perhaps. Perhaps. But let's take it slowly. I'll call you.' I was placing my words carefully. 'Very soon. And we will talk. But this is right out of the blue, Jim. Give a little time please. We'll speak.'

He seemed not to disagree. I hung up. He knows nothing about children, I thought. Well, that's probably to my advantage.

*

At lunchtime I went up to the Three Johns in Islington to meet Cooper. I'd always fancied arranging to meet three guys called John there and having a cheap laugh. Anyway. No Johns, just one Ben.

He looked much the same as he always had, plump and benevolent with a very clean neck. He wasn't in uniform. His idea of plain clothes were the kind that shriek 'plain clothes' at you. 'Slacks', 'Sports Jacket', that kind of thing. At least I assume that's what they are. Not really my kind of wardrobe. He was there at a tiny round table in the corner, looking almost actively innocuous. 'Oh, no, don't look at me,' his posture cried out, 'I'm really not interesting at all.' It makes you wonder how he got as far as he has.

'Well, hel-lo,' he said, with a chummy emphasis on the 'lo'. He made as if to stand up but obviously wasn't going to. He'd have knocked the table over for one, and anyway he only wanted to make a show of politeness, not actually to be polite. 'What'll you have?' he said. 'Cider still?'

One of Cooper's creepiest habits is that he remembers everything, even the tiniest things. It must have been three years since I'd seen him, and he remembered I drank cider. He'd have made a great gossip columnist. It obviously helped in a policeman too.

I sat on a childish urge to order something else entirely – partly because I couldn't think immediately of anything else to order that wouldn't carry some other connotation. Anything non-alcoholic and he'd know I had a hangover, and I just didn't want him knowing anything about me, even that. Vodka? He'd think I'd gone dipso. Beer? He'd think I'd gone dyke. Cinzano? He'd think I'd gone off my trolley. What's the opposite of cider anyway? And then I sat on an even more childish urge to say 'No, let me get them', which would just have made him laugh up his acrylic sleeve to think that it was that important to me not to be indebted to him. Which considering what I'd come for was a bad joke. I had a half of cider.

First he wanted to make small talk. What was I riding now, he said. That uncanny police perspicacity at work again – I'd come in wearing thin cotton trousers, a cotton shirt and lace-up sandals like a Roman soldier's; no leather, no helmet, no nothing. I told him I wasn't riding bikes any more.

'Why's that then? Trying to lead a clean life?' he said wittily. Cooper has this *idée fixe* that owning, riding or even thinking too much about motorcycles is an indictable offence. This despite the fact that he rides one.

'Doctor's orders,' I said. I wasn't going to point out to him the elongated map of scars on my left leg where many talented doctors had poked their fingers and scalpels and helpful metal pins in an attempt to restore it to something like a useful condition. They did their job well. It works OK now. Pretty much. Nor did I tell him about Lily, and my absolute unwillingness to put her little body, or mine for her sake, anywhere near anything cold or hard or loud or sharp or dirty.

'Heard you had a smash,' he said. 'Would have thought it would take more than that to put you off.' I smiled. Not a big smile. I've been given that line so often that I have no problem at all about feeling absolutely no need to explain myself.

'Lucky you didn't smash up last night,' he continued. Ah. To business. I reined in my impatience and pulled my eyes up to meet his. This was not the time to stand on details like what had actually happened. My dignity was not the point – my licence was.

'That would've cost a lot more.' He let me stew on that

for a moment or two. 'But as it is,' he said, pulling himself up on his chair, 'you're in luck. This one's on me.'

I looked at him blankly. If he meant what it sounded as if he meant I didn't understand. Why would he do that? There could be no earthly reason why he should. There could be no earthly reason that I would be glad to hear about, anyway.

'HGT 425Q,' he said. It didn't help my blankness.

'Pontiac Firebird,' he said. 'Eight-cylinder 455, fully-powered, nineteen sixty-nine or seventy but Q registered . . .'

A little recognition must have crept into my eyes.

'. . . when it was imported from New Orleans in 1986 and still so registered . . .'

And a little more.

'. . . illegally, as it happens, and, as it happens, in your name.'

I couldn't see why he was interested in dredging up an ancient bit of registration bureaucracy. Of course, if you bring a car in from the States you are meant to have it registered as a Q only until you can find out the exact six months in which it was first registered in the States, rather than just the year which is all they need over there. But nobody ever gets round to it. There are hundreds of vehicles going round on Q plates and nobody gives a damn.

And anyway, I knew the car, but it wasn't mine. It never had been. Harry Makins had registered it in my name years ago because he had so many old wrecks registered in his own, at his own address, that he was afraid some officious official would work out that he was a dealer and come around demanding to see his insurance and his tax papers and his fire precautions and whether or not he had a window in the room where he kept his electric kettle. Or so he had said. So I had said, of course, register it to me, no problem. I had been under the impression that I was in love at the time, and it had amused me to have a car in my name when the nearest I had ever come to driving anything with four wheels was the dodgems on Shepherds Bush Green. And anyway, he'd junked the car within months, taken the engine out to put it in a classic Oldsmobile – a Rocket 88 if I remember right – and had a breaker's yard haul away the remains. At least that was what I'd heard. And it hadn't been parked outside my building any more. I had been living in Clerkenwell at the time: a narrow Georgian house full of despatch riders, a few doors down from Charles Dickens.

But Harry and I had broken up soon after . . . so what do I know, I found myself thinking.

Cooper was looking at me.

'It's all coming back, isn't it?' he said kindly.

I put what I hoped was a look of innocent confusion on my face. 'The Pontiac,' I said. 'Of course. I'd completely forgotten. I only had it for, oh . . . a couple of weeks. Anyway it's been junked now.'

'Really?' he said. 'And when was that?'

'Eighty-eight?' I said. 'Maybe eighty-seven?'

'Oh,' said Cooper, in that tone of whimsical sarcastic

disbelief that you'd think only policemen on the telly use. 'That's funny.'

I wasn't going to say anything more until I knew what he was getting at. I am not a person who by nature lies to policemen, but I find a quietly uninformative courtesy is normally least trouble to all concerned when you don't know what the hell's going on. Unfortunately, Cooper seemed to have the same idea. I looked at him politely, he looked at me politely. Mexican standoff at the Three Johns.

Well, all I wanted was to give him the five hundred pounds that was burning a hole in my pocket and get his word that his infallible system for the disposal of unwanted drink-driving charges was on my case. I had no desire to get into a discussion about a car that as far as I knew had been squished into a little metal cube and buried in some slagheap in the Essex flatlands. He looked at me, I looked at him.

'Eddie Bates,' he said.

'Who's Eddie Bates?' I said, in totally genuine and relieved ignorance. Whatever it was he wanted, I couldn't help him. I'd never heard of any Eddie Bates.

'Of Pelham Crescent SW7,' he said. Blank.

'Outside which address Pontiac Firebird HGT 425Q has been observed on twelve separate occasions in the past two months. Averaging one and a half times a week. A regular caller.'

'Ben,' I said, leaning over the table in an open and friendly fashion. 'You've lost me. I don't know anyone rich enough to live round there. I don't go to Joseph or the Conran shop. The last time I set foot in South Ken I was eight years old, visiting the dinosaurs with twenty of my little schoolfriends. I haven't seen that car since nineteen eighty-seven and I've never heard of any Eddie Bates.'

He gave me his clean, steady look. An innocent-looking look, trying to judge innocence. He decided to believe me. I think.

'How it works is this,' he said finally. 'The reason your little misdemeanour last night is not going to be pressed is because I let on that me and my section just happen to be keeping an eye on you in connection with something else entirely which is none of the business of the little street copper who so efficiently picked you up. Your paperwork comes to me and I open a file in your name and pop the papers in and there they stay till kingdom come or till that other case entirely comes to court, whichever is sooner.'

'Clever,' I said. I'd been wondering, actually.

'But,' he said.

I looked at him politely.

'There's already a file in your name.'

I felt a little slow.

'You actually are under surveillance.'

Alarm was just a tiny, vicious twist in my belly. Anger was swift to follow. I said nothing.

'You're not being watched and followed around. We haven't got that kind of manpower,' he said. 'But your car, and your name, are significant in a situation that we are most certainly watching. Now I don't know why it's so important to you not to lose your licence, but I imagine the same reasons might hold if it came to being connected with Eddie Bates.'

'Ben, I don't know the man . . .'

'So you said. That's irrelevant. The point is that you are in a position to . . .'

I rather feared I was.

'. . . and if you *were* to I would consider it a great personal favour.'

My heart sank. I had a horrible feeling I had no choice.

'You've got no choice,' he said.

THREE

Us Then

What he wanted me to do was, as he put it, 'chum up to Harry Makins'. He knew perfectly well the Pontiac was Harry's. He was unimpressed when I told him I hadn't seen Harry since the winter of 1988 and my last view of him was obscured by a chair he was throwing out the window at me. I was to chum up with Harry and chum up with Eddie Bates and await further instructions. That was it.

Chum up with Harry. Chum up with Harry. Like, what, ring him? After eight years? Out of the blue? Hey, Harry!

*

I first met him in a bar, of course. Janie, a Cynthia Heimel fan, said that I'd never meet my dream man in a bar, because my dream man had better things to do than hang around drinking. This wasn't that kind of bar, though – it was the kind where people hang around drinking on expenses and call it a meeting, a place in Soho full of Mexican beer, sharp, fleshy foliage and men with silly hair.

I noticed Harry because he looked completely wrong. No Paul Smith suit, no pony tail, no eyes leaping to the door at every entrance. He was too naturally cool for such a posy place. He wore his leathers like only very long skinny people can: as if he had been born with one skin too few, and the leather was it, filling the body out to its right and harmonious proportions. Also, he looked very slightly dangerous. Very slightly.

He came in with a bunch of Paul Smiths as I was sitting at the bar, and after some brief backchat wanted to know was that my bike outside – I was in leathers too – because if so he had some blue-dot rear-light covers one of which would probably do for it if I was interested in that kind of thing.

As it happened that's just the kind of thing I was interested in in those days, and as they are not usually available in this country and as (as I told him) I didn't know you could even get them for a 1963 Dynaglide (same year as me – one reason I bought it) I said yes, and had taken his phone number before he leaned forward and whispered rather cosily, I thought, considering the brevity of our acquaintance, into my ear: 'Just checking. You can't get them for the Dynaglide. But I had to know you weren't a git.'

And then as I leaned back a little and turned round a little to look at him, he said, 'Can I just kiss you now? It would save so much time . . .'

Yee-hah! So I said, 'You can kiss me now and then not again for a month.' So he did, and we had this fantastic snog in the middle of the pretentious bar and when he let me go (yes *he* let *me* go) five minutes later my knees wobbled slightly as I leant back against my tall stool.

'I've got to go and see a man about a Chevrolet,' he said. 'I'll see you four weeks from Saturday at Gossips.' And then before I could sneer at his cheek the barman said, 'You Angeline? Mr Herbert'll see you now,' and I had to go because I too was there on business.

'Mr Herbert?' Harry said, laughing, as he turned away. 'You a waitress, or what?'

'No, I'm a belly dancer,' I replied. The grin that split Harry's face was something to see. 'Belly dancer on a Harley?' he said. 'Oh, *yes*!'

Gossips. Harry and I used to go there every week and dance in revoltingly sexual fashion to the slinky reggae. I'd do a camel walk to Gregory Isaacs. Harry loved that place. Perhaps he still goes there.

*

Saturday night I got Brigid in to look after Lily, and headed up west on the bus. I might need to drink.

I leapt off at Oxford Circus just after closing time, into a crowd of disconsolate tourists with no clue what happens in London when the pubs are shut. I cut through Soho, passing one of the Greek restaurants where I used to dance all those years ago. The fairy lights were glittering round its steamed-up window, and I knew if I went in Andreas would be there, fatter than ever in his cummerbund, and he'd give me a big smelly hug and gaze at me with such sympathy in his fat brown eyes and say, 'How is leg, my darling, how is leg?' Well, I can leap off buses, and cart a three-year-old around, and camel-walk to make her laugh, but I'll never wriggle for a living again and that is that. Nothing to say on the subject so I don't pop in to be hugged by Andreas.

You may wonder why I was a belly dancer. You probably think belly dancing is a joke. I really hate to explain things – especially myself – but I'll try.

When I was sixteen my Egyptian friend Zeinab and I absconded from home one night (hers was strict, mine wasn't) to go out with some naughty cousins of hers who were eighteen and rather rich. They were fresh from Cairo and not used to girls who went out and drank. They took us to an expensive but deeply tacky Arab nightclub where we all got slaughtered among the smoked glass, much to the disapproval of the *maitre d'* who had my companions down as the fallen generation, shaming their families and their country and their religion – in which he wasn't far wrong. As for me, I was just a no-good *Farangi* bint, so what would you expect. He wasn't in the least surprised when, after the floorshow – a belly dancer, of course – ended, I got up and imitated her. He was surprised that I wasn't altogether atrocious. I was amazed – not that I was any good, because I wasn't, and wouldn't have known anyway, but by how completely lovely the movements felt. He said – with an eye to having a sixteen-year-old blonde working at the club – would I like to come back and audition. The boys thought it very funny. Zeinab said I could, but I would have to learn how to dance properly first, and she would have to come with me. So I became a cabaret-style belly dancer without knowing a thing about it.

Not knowing is a situation I have never liked, so I found things out. Took classes, talked to the other girls, persuaded Zeinab to help me out on the cultural stuff. She taught me a few smart retorts in Arabic to remind the boys that though I was blonde, a foreigner and half-naked I still deserved a little respect. (My favourite is *'Mafeesh'*, 'you're not getting any'.) There were problems. Like the time I innocently expressed to the other girls my desire that a man in the audience would be so moved by my performance that he would empty a bottle of champagne over *me,* as I had seen happen to a girl at another club.

'Habibti,' said Aisha, who was at least forty and looked after the little ones, as she termed us. 'He does that to show that he has bought her for the night.'

Initially I just loved the movements and the music, the pause after the introduction before the *takasim*, the solo, would take off, the slow slow changes of mood. I loved the *nay* – the flute. The *nay* transported me. Still does. The moment before the player takes his breath, when my stillness would be perfect, and the moment of shifting . . . the music is visible. I'd learnt ballet – how to be stiff and fake and eternally fleshlessly prepubescent and unnatural – and had given it up because I'd grown tits. This was something else: it was something my newly female body felt at home in, not ridiculed by like ballet. And I loved the fact that I could make lots of money, and hell yes I loved the glamour, and the men fancying me (though I kept my distance) and the other girls with their mysterious lives, and I loved the fact that I didn't tell my parents I was doing it. Hassan, the manager, soon leant that I wasn't always drunk, and that to have me at all he had to put up with my conditions, which were that I would work only one night a week, Friday or Saturday, and that I had to be home by one. I don't think he knew that these incorporated my parents' conditions on my social life, and allowed me one night a week where I could go to parties and watch Janie getting off with boys and pay for our taxi home.

And I loved not thinking. All week at school doing differentiation and the causes of the First World War, Saturday night just being in my body. Just like John Travolta.

When I was at university I used to come down to London at weekends to dance. I paid my own way – finally I told the parents, and they took it. Aisha told me she still hadn't told hers, because dancing was such a low profession. That made me feel bad. I was a secure girl, playing. I knew my parents wouldn't like it but nobody was going to shoot me or be shamed. I'd passed all my exams, hadn't I?

Later I learnt about the symbolic significance of the veil, of revelation and concealment; about Ishtar, the Babylonian goddess of love, a virgin who took lovers, symbol of both chastity and fertility, and how when her husband Tammuz died she went in search of him, down through the seven times seven gates of the underworld. At every seventh gate she gave up one of her veils and one of her jewels as the price of admission, tempting and seducing the guards into letting her through. By the last gate she was naked. It was called the dance of Shalome, of Welcome. Salome was named after it when she did it for Herod. I learnt about Demeter resting at the Well of the Beautiful Dances at Eleusis, during her wanderings in search of Persephone (after whom she too went down into the Underworld) and about the Eleusinian Mystery dances, and about the woman called Baubo – belly – who danced for Demeter and made her laugh. I read Carlo Suares's commentary on the Song of Songs, about the Shulamite – same root as Shalom – and his alternative translation, which had her as a dancer. I learnt that seven was the number of the universe, because the ancient Mesopotamians, who knew most about that kind of thing, knew of seven planets. I loved all that stuff. But I was just a cabaret dancer. I pierced my navel to wear a fake jewel in it. Do you know why a belly dancer should have a ruby in her tummy? Because in the 1930s and '40s in Hollywood, when a belly-dancing scene in a biblical epic was a good excuse to get some female flesh on the screen, the navel could not be shown. Too erogenous. So stick a ruby in it.

I was just a London girl, with a part-time job and a

weakness for large motorcycles and the ancient and universal roots of belly dancing. That's what I was then.

Harry wasn't at Gossips, of course. Why should he be? After all this time, just hanging round there waiting for me to look in. I ordered a vodka and tonic and looked around at the relics of a life I no longer lived. All that smoke, all that noise, strangers to me now that I lived in baby-land. You don't think it'll happen to you but it does. If the infant wants the fridge door to be adorned with plastic letters of the alphabet, and admiring them keeps the kid occupied for ten minutes when you want a cup of tea and a look at the paper, believe me dignity goes out the window and plastic letters of the alphabet go up on the fridge door. If the infant has eczema and the doctor says smoking around her makes it worse, you stop smoking round her. If George Jones makes the infant laugh and Skunk Anansie makes her cry, then you put on the George Jones. And sooner or later Skunk Anansie sounds ugly and loud to you too, and cigarette smoke is more than you can bear. It's a damn shame. There I was, fully equipped for a night out, babysittered up, and I didn't like what I used to like.

A black man at the other end of the bar was looking at me. I turned away from him and stared out to the dance-floor, glimpsing ghosts among the dancers. Harry and I, intertwined. Janie looning about, shimmying her bum out of time and waving her arms like an Indian warrior goddess. She never could dance. Janie and me laughing and Harry not knowing why. Harry and me laughing and Janie sulking because she didn't want to be a gooseberry.

I could feel the man coming towards me, so I was prepared when I heard him speak. 'Old timer,' he said, in the particular hoarse voice of someone accustomed to making themselves heard above loud music. 'Angeline, init?'

I turned round and squinted at him. Familiarity took its time to seep into my brain. A neat number two now gleamed where shaggy locks used to hang, and a rather tidy shirt covered up what I realized I had never seen in anything other than a string vest, but there was no mistaking the teeth. Dizzy Ansah, as I live and breathe.

'Hey, Dizzy,' I said, with some genuine pleasure.

'My man,' he said, inaccurately but affectionately.

'What happened to the hair?' I couldn't help it. His hair used to be a major topographical feature of Notting Hill: a fair three feet of big, clean, good locks. No onion bhajis on Dizzy. They were the best-kept, best-looking and best-loved-by-their-owner locks in W11 . His devotion to them was only one of the things that made him so boring.

'Put me in a box, man. People see your hair, think they know who you are. Got fed up of that box, right, wanted to fly up out of it, float around a bit, see the world, before I landed down in some other box, maybe fit me better. How you doing, man?'

So then it was easy. Easy to mention Harry, easy to find that Dizzy used the same gym as him (Harry uses a gym?), easy to say I was here every Saturday, easy to mention how jolly it would be to see Harry after all these years. If Dizzy was still the gossip he used to be, and if Harry was half the man I thought him, I would either get a phone call or see him here next week.

*

Going home on the night bus I wondered what man was it, that I thought Harry to be? And if I thought that of him, how come it ended with a chair flying out the window?

Harry was a wideboy. 'Yeah,' he'd say, flashing his grin. 'Don't always fit in the lift.' Harry was in the motor trade. Harry knew everything. For example: I knew I didn't have to give Dizzy my number. I was ex-directory – not because I'm flash, but because there's an old old tradition of not knowing the difference between a belly dancer and a prostitute (I should know, I did my dissertation on it) – but Harry would find my number. Harry had energy and guts and morals and we lived together – more or less, he never gave up his flat – for three years. And we had a blast.

I can't remember what the row was about.

Oh, yes, I can.

He was never jealous or pissed off about my work. Then one night . . .

I was booked to dance at Shiraz, one of my regular spots, a Lebanese restaurant just north of Oxford Street. It's calm, classy and intensely wealthy. Exquisitely dressed obsidian-haired diners greet each other with 'salaam'; rows of lanterns throw patterned shadows and jewel-coloured light. I liked it there. You could sit at the bar beforehand

and drink a tiny coffee and nobody gave you grief. Ali let me change in his office, not like most places where you're in the loo, washing your feet in the sink and trying to dry your hair under the hand-drier. I was wearing the green and gold. How it floods back.

Zayra and Noor were there, so damned glamorous they looked like transvestites. Noor had just been sacked for dancing too rudely: God, you should have seen her, licking her fingers, writhing on the floor, hands down inside her belt. I don't mind floorwork – the Indian temple priestesses, the Yakshini, were doing floorwork in the fifth century B.C., but that was for God not Mammon, and there has to be some kind of line between dancing and pornography. The girls were giving me fish-eyed looks: to them rival really means rival. They'd spent too long in the Arab clubs, where you have to hostess as well, and do your second spot at four in the morning. You were sitting there from ten till four with nothing to do except chat up the punters, so if you didn't want to you were fucked. Half the time if you did want to you were fucked too. Half the time that's what the girls wanted anyway. The money was good and the dancing was just an advertisement. Well, that's part of the tradition too. There was a tribe in Algeria – the Ouled Nail – who brought up their daughters to dance and whore from the age of twelve: they would travel from oasis to oasis around the Sahara, till they had saved enough money for their dowry, then they'd marry and bring up their daughters just the same. The French had a whale of a time with them in the nineteenth century. I met some of their great-great-granddaughters in Biskra, after I ran away from Harry. They were still wearing massive feathers in their tiaras and about five dresses each. They were sorry for me with my meagre single dress, and offered me a few of their own to make me decent. Their dance was so different from the cabaret stuff you see in London, and to the languorous Egyptian form, and to the Moroccan Chikats. Those girls could instruct their muscles individually. They visibly, violently, pulsed muscles that I don't even have. That's where I learnt to wriggle one breast at a time.

Noor was murdered. They never found who did it. Didn't care, I think. As they don't when it's a prostitute. Or a dancer. Well, you know, not a virgin. Probably. And you know, she was brown, nearly black, so really, so what? When they find a nice pink schoolgirl in a ditch you never hear the end of it. But Noor merited only a quick flurry of press attention, just enough for the front pages of the tabloids to use the studio photos she'd had done to try and get an agent. Little Noor, drop-dead gorgeous in her sexy chiffon outfit, her twenty-year-old body on display, Miss pouting exotic erotic. No family that cared to claim her. I think she was Pakistani originally. She was a bitch, but from what I knew of her life it wasn't surprising.

So that night: Ahmed and the band started up – live music here, a luxury – and I swept on to the floor, completely ignoring the waiters, who were possibly the world's most talented men, the way they danced around me carrying their precarious three-storey puddings with sparklers on top. Then I'm up on the table, kebab-hopping. I play to every diner at every table, circling the men's heads with my snakey wriggling arms; clicking my little finger cymbals for the children (they love us, they think we're that Princess Jasmine out of *Aladdin*); grinning at the women, who discuss my technique among themselves. The women tip better than the men, half the time. Belly dancing started out, after all, as a fertility dance for the Goddess, before any of these male religions started in. Then when the Goddess was banned and women put away, it evolved in the harem, as a dance by women for women. It was done as exercise for pregnancy. The belly-rippling movements imitate the contractions of labour as much as those of sexual abandon. Then the men cottoned on, and took to peeking through the silken curtains, wanting for themselves one of the few pure joys that permeate that harem miasma of tension and boredom. At the Topkapi harem in Istanbul during the Turkish Empire, cucumbers were delivered ready chopped, in case the women tried to amuse themselves. Only a few years ago fundamentalists in Egypt suggested banning aubergines altogether. God, what we might do with them! In some countries, the same Arabic word, *fitna,* can mean chaos, disaster and sexual desire for a woman, and hence the beautiful woman herself.

But that night: within half an hour my jewelled cleavage and glittering waistband were erupting with sweat-dampened five- and ten-pound notes. It was a good night, and it didn't go wrong until Harry came into Ali's office when I was changing back in civvies.

He was meant to be taking me over to Soho for another booking. Why wasn't I on the bike? Don't know. Can't remember. Once we were in the car he started in. He said he'd had it up to here and he couldn't stand it and had I no respect and all kinds of stuff like that. He said the girls were nothing more than whores and if I thought I could get away with not being one I was a bloody fool and he couldn't stand by and let any woman of his – and I quote – make a living shaking her arse because any way you shake it it's the same damn thing.

I begged to differ.

He drove me straight back to his house (thus jeopardizing one of my regular jobs) and told me he wasn't a fool.

I told him I had never taken him for a fool.

He said if I didn't know what was going on, then I must be a fool.

I said I knew perfectly well that some of the girls worked as strippers too, and that some of them were on the game.

'You know about it,' he said.

'Yes,' I said. 'Of course I do. I'm not blind and I'm not stupid.'

'And you think it's all right.'

'Of course I don't think it's all right. But I can't tell people what to do,' I said. 'It's not right for me. But, you know, I'm not my sister's keeper.'

'You know about it.'

His face had changed. It changed colour, went hard and difficult. Then he launched into a sort of frenzy of fury, anger such as I had never seen. I didn't really know what I was being accused of. I thought he thought I was turning tricks – but he seemed to believe I wasn't. I couldn't believe he thought I was. He knew me. He knew I loved him. He knew – oh, God, he knew lots of things, but he was acting as if he didn't know any of them.

Actually, he was frightening me. So I left. And he threw the chair out the window. I went round to Janie's on the tube, still clutching my plastic bag of dancing frock.

'Harry's lost his marbles,' I said, and burst into tears.

She crawled out of bed, made tea, hugged me, wanted to know what it was all about. I told her the gist and she started crying too. 'How could he?' she kept saying. 'How could he think that of you? How could he?' She was gratifyingly upset on my behalf.

I tried to ring him but there was no answer.

'Can I stay here?' I asked, and so I did, wearing her T-shirt and sharing her bed. I couldn't face the despatch riders and their laddish sympathy. Janie kept funny hours so half the time the bed was occupied in shifts. I kept funny hours myself and didn't really notice where she was. But she looked after me. We had twice-daily sessions where I would update her on how many times I had rung and got only his voice on the answering machine, on who else I had tried, on where I had left messages, and confirming that no, he hadn't rung back. I carried on working, dancing with all the allure of a worn-out j-cloth. After four days I went round to his flat and picked up some clothes that had emigrated there as things do when you half live together. He wasn't there – I'd hoped he would be. I rang mutual friends, who hadn't seen him. To say my world was falling apart would not be an exaggeration.

I rang, I went round, I wrote to him. I rang his mother even, and God help me I swallowed my pride and rang each of his four sisters and two brothers, including Jason with whom he wasn't on speaking terms. Then I kissed Janie and told her to be good, climbed on the bike and rode to Gibraltar, where I looked across at the Atlas mountains and decided not to go home for a while.

FOUR

Tea with Jim

But that was in another country, and besides the wench has changed. Now, and in England, there is no 'not going home for a while'. Home exists. Home is not just me, wherever I happen to put myself. It's my loved and protected place, my own little sceptred isle. I built it on the safest ground I could recover, in that panicky time, dreaming and lecturing myself in images of trees and compost and roots and how the rigid dies and the flexible survives, but the earth must be good when the winds are high. For six months I had the same Elvis song on my mind: I'm not an oak, I'm a willow, I can bend. Things will shift around you anyway, whatever you do, and you must allow for it. I always thought, in my girlish dreams, that safe ground was love, romantic married love, the everyday realistic kind, and that from that ground grew roses round the door. Perhaps it is and they do. I wouldn't know.

But I know what safe ground is not. Safe ground is not what I have. What I have is not safe ground. Despite the true true love in my house, underpinning is constantly necessary. You cannot underpin your house with falsehood. Well, of course you can't. So you must do it with truth. No matter that you don't like the truth. No matter that I don't like the fact that Jim is Lily's father, or that he wants to see her. No matter that I don't like him.

So my first response to Jim's request, straight anger at him, was neither here nor there. Jim is a fact, Jim is not doing anything wrong in the long run. Wrong by me, yes, but not actually wrong. Which made me even angrier.

No mention of the three years I have fed her, paid for her, loved her. No mention of the first six months when I couldn't really walk, and of what my parents did for us then. No mention of why he never wanted her to be with him before. No mention of his complete lack of interest in her – oh, no, he sent her a present once. A bottle of Postman Pat bubble bath. He doesn't even know she has eczema. Doesn't even know she can't even use soap without her skin erupting into an unbearable heat and itching that has her trying to claw it off, and raking flakes off beneath her fingernails. Hasn't heard the crunching sound of compulsive midnight scratching. Doesn't know that I change her sheets every day when it's bad. Hasn't seen the bloodstains, the tiny scars made by four little nails tearing, a miniature bear's claw, on her shoulders and her legs and her arms. Doesn't even know that it's quite hard to explain to a two-year-old (as she was) why she can't have her present. I poured out the bubble bath and put her medicinal bath oil in the bottle. But it wasn't pink. Oh, the tragedies of small lives. I considered adding cochineal. But would that make her skin worse? Or dye her pink? I made her a pink mermaid tail, covered with sequins like a dance costume. I killed her mother.

*

I had followed Neil's advice. Jim never turned up at the hospital. Mum and I sat there waiting for him, talking through what Neil had said.

'I should look after her, shouldn't I?' I said. Mum said I needed looking after myself.

'In the long run.'

'We'll all go home, and we'll all see how it goes,' said Mum. Sometimes she gets firm. Sometimes her little fears drop away and in the face of something big, she becomes big. She was a teacher. She can make me feel like a little child.

'Your father and I will make the parental responsibility application, and we'll all stay put a while, and when things have settled we'll see how they settle. It'll be better coming from a couple.'

'Why can't we just have her!'

'We can't because we can't. She's the law's. But they'll see it our way. Neil says we have a good chance. Don't you worry, not now.'

They were still telling me to rest my leg when I lost all my patience in a rush, and hobbled upstairs to the baby unit, soul racing on ahead, and said, Look, can she come out, please, please, please, is she ready, can we take her? Mum and Dad came up after me. A nice kind devoted family, trying to triumph over tragedy, wanting to take their baby home.

Mum had been in every day. The nurses liked her. The doctors liked her. They felt, as much as hospital staff can allow themselves to feel, for our tragedy. One little junior nurse cried whenever she saw Lily and had to be moved to a different ward. So Mum was there and I was there and Dad was there and Jim was not.

Neil said he had seen him, and he had not heard about what had happened. It seemed unbelievable. Apparently he had sobered up and imagined that Janie was taking a break and decided to let her stew a little before fetching her home. It had happened before. I think he was glad it had happened then – gave him an excuse not to be around for the birth. Like so many hard men, Jim can't take anything really hard.

Neil said I was never again to ask him not to tell someone something. 'Your girlfriend's dead, by the way, only I'm not meant to tell you.' Well, Jim must have found out sooner or later.

I was all for just taking her, once she was off her tubes. I was going to sneak upstairs on my crutches, tuck her inside my leather jacket, and ride her home on the Harley with my sick leg dangling in the wind. Never mind that the Harley was a write-off, that I could hardly walk, that the hospital authorities would chase me up, that it was a truly idiotic scheme. I was on drugs. It seemed a great idea to me. Mum repeated her mantra. Neil said no, and organized a little meeting at the hospital.

We sat in a greenish room. Pigeons were nesting somewhere outside the aquarium windows and their babies' caterwauling sounded like serial murder. There were fag ends on the floor and plastic chairs that you couldn't wrest apart from each other. My leg hurt. Mum looked as if she were in shock, Dad looked determined, Neil looked worried. God knows what I looked like.

We told them that Jim was out of the picture, not interested. He hasn't even been here, we said. They said they would have to make inquiries, let him know. We said why? Anyway he does know. He knows she was pregnant. He knows how long pregnancy takes. He knows our phone numbers. If he's interested let him come and ask. It's not as if they were married. What rights did he have? They said someone had to find out. We said let whoever is interested find out. We said that formal adoption procedures were being put into place. We said that Mum and Dad had applied for parental responsibility under the Children Act 1989. We said the court would sort it all out but in the meantime Lily should be with her granny. Neil blinded them with legal science. They were understaffed. We were there. Dolores kissed me as we left.

So we took Lily home, and she was ours. A member of our family. Out into the world, out of intensive care, safe and to remain so. The only fly was when Jim rang me, a month after she was born, the day we got home to Mum's.

'Hello, Angeline,' he said, sounding serious and sober. I could just picture him: clean shirt, clean-shaven, his bog-brush hair brushed, his face pink. Jim is a very big man and specializes in bonhomie. He used to wear tartan trousers when he was younger, but he doesn't think it appropriate any more. He used to be quite funny before he got a job and started taking himself seriously. He's quite good at his computers apparently. Men like him; women find him attractive, even now – well, then – when his face was already going a bit blobby. He worked out, but the flesh was creeping up though he was only, what, thirty-three. When he's angry his face goes red and he shouts and shouts and shouts. He's a bully. He drinks too much and cries when he apologizes. I don't imagine that he's changed. I'd like to be able to tell you what Janie saw in him but I don't really know.

'Hello, Jim,' I said. I was quivering. Anger and fear. It's a bad combination.

'I suppose we ought to talk,' he said.

'Don't see why,' I said.

'It's mine, you know,' he said.

'It?' I said. 'Yeah.'

'I heard it was a girl.'

'Yes,' I said. 'She is.'

'She'll need to be registered,' he said.

'Yeah,' I said. I was so glad Mum hadn't answered the phone. She didn't know the half of it, but she knew enough.

'Call her Jane,' he said.

'Fuck off,' I said. Janie had chosen Lily. Lily for a girl, Edward for a boy. If he didn't know that he didn't deserve to know.

'Well,' he said.

I said nothing.

'I don't know why you're being so high and . . . sorry,' he said.

I said nothing.

'You'll have to put my name on the birth certificate,' he said.

I said nothing. Then, 'yes'.

Well. It was true. You can't dodge truth. Janie didn't. And I can't.

'I insist,' he said.

'I said yes,' I said.

He began to blurt: 'Look, it's not been easy for . . .'

I hung up.

Mum was furious when I told her. Dad nearly blew a fuse. He stormed out of the house, and came back half an hour later saying, 'She's right, you know.'

'It doesn't seem right,' said Mum. But it was true. So.

*

So I rang Jim the morning after I saw Dizzy and told him he could come. I told him I would not tell Lily that he was her father. I asked him as a favour not to tell her himself.

'Just come and see her, see how it goes, see what is going to happen, and tell her later. If you bugger off again how will it be for her?' ('Yes, you have a daddy, here's your daddy, oh, yes, but you won't be seeing him again.' This is me fantasizing about the result I *want*, for God's sake. The best possible result.)

'What's the point of that?' he wanted to know. I tried to explain.

'Angie,' he said, 'I'm not doing this on a whim. I want to do it. I'm not going to disappear again. Three years is a long time and things have changed. I'm her father and I want to be her father. It's not anything personal against you and if you could stop being so prickly for a moment and work with me for Lily's benefit . . .' (He's had counselling. He's been talking to a social worker or something. That's not his voice.) '. . . I would tell you that I appreciate everything you've done for her . . .' (*he* appreciates what I've done? It's not for him to appreciate that . . . who is he to appreciate what is done for Lily?) '. . . but things are going to change now. I'm sorry if it upsets you. I have every right to . . . visit my daughter and I intend to use that right. And my wife is coming too.'

Wife.

It occurred to me that it might be a good idea to make notes of our telephone calls, of what he said. Perhaps even tape them.

'I'll tell her that friends of Janie's are coming. Please don't tell her you're her father.'

'You're asking me to lie to her.'

'Please don't tell her. She'd be upset.'

We arranged that they would come on Wednesday at four. This was Sunday. Just coming to tea.

*

Cooper kept ringing me wanting to know how I was doing. I started to hate the answerphone. I told him I was on the case but I wasn't. I was starting to think that I really didn't like what was going on. Not to fuss about it, of course not. I don't fuss. Usually. I just get on with things. That's what women do. Then occasionally you start to feel a little powerless. My least favourite feeling.

I made the mistake of trying to imagine what Jim was going to do. Wasted a lot of energy that way when I should have been concentrating, getting some work done.

I did become something else after the accident. I put together all the notes and things I'd written when I was in North Africa, dragged out my intellect from where I'd parked it after doing my degree, and wrote a book about the history and culture of Arab dance through western eyes. It was full of beautiful pictures and wild stories and did rather well, and now I am known to be the person who knows about belly dancing, harems, women in Islam, Orientalism and almost anything else in that direction that a journalist in need of a quote, or a researcher in need of a radio guest, might want. I work from home, my time is my own and I make a decent living.

Why do I feel I am writing this down in an affidavit?

*

Lily was on edge. I think she smelt it. She was excited about the visit. Friends of Mummy's!

'People who knew her, and want to see you. But you know lots of people who knew her, Granny and Grandpa and everyone . . .'

You can't lie to children. It's one of the great true cliches. She knew damn well this was important, because she saw it in my face and heard it in my voice.

They arrived exactly on time. Jim looked older, fatter, more unpleasant. There's a certain nasty look that prosperity gives to some faces, and he had it. The wife was small and dark with neat hair. Early thirties, well looked after. I couldn't make her out. She looked almost as if there were nothing to her – nothing to make her herself, rather than just anyone. Just small, neat, dark femininity. A sort of cipher, in expensive clothes.

I showed them into the kitchen. I had thought so hard about this and now all I could think was, 'I wish we'd met somewhere else'. I felt a profound unease at not being able to read the wife at all.

'My wife,' said Jim. 'Nora.'

Nora. Nora. Well that tells me nothing at all. Hey, stranger, who the hell are you and what are you doing here?

She smiled, a closed smile. I put the kettle on. What else?

Lily was upstairs. She'd said she didn't want to come down because some friends of her teddy's mummy were coming round. I called her. I was Judas. That woman there replaced my sister in this creep's affections and they want you . . . I don't know what they want of you but they want you.

Lily came down slowly, bringing the teddy, looking at the floor.

Jim's face was set, still.

Nora looked up at her and started to laugh.

'Oh, what a little darling!' she exclaimed. Lily is a darling. A dark golden creature, with long dark hair and curving golden cheeks. She's quite like an animal: furry, tempestuous on occasion. Clever, kind, but won't be patronized. I suppose she got her darkness from Jim, but the quality of it was so different. His is Celtic, hers is like blondeness made dark. Like honey.

'Hello, Lily,' said Jim. He held his arms out as if to hug her. Nora leaned forward to take her arm. These fuckwits know nothing about children. Lily went behind my legs, twining like a cat. I sent her 'hate them' messages through my knees, and regretted them, and didn't regret them. It is wrong to make a child hate her father. With any luck she'll hate him of her own accord.

Nora looked at me as if she expected me to shoo Lily off my legs and into their arms. Expect on, sunshine. I did nothing. Lily twined, and wanted to climb me. I picked her up, put her on my hip, went to a chair on the far side of the table, and pushed a plate of biscuits towards them. What the hell do they expect?

'What a beautiful little girl,' said Nora again. Lily didn't look at her. Jim looked as if he couldn't believe that I wasn't even going to say 'come on, darling', as mothers do whenever they ask their children to betray themselves.

Nora was flummoxed. She looked at Jim. Jim looked at me. Nora looked at me. Lily looked at the stitching on my shirt. Almost visibly, Nora fell back and regrouped.

'I brought you a present,' she said to Lily's back. Oh, so it's going to be like that.

The present, like the clothes, was expensive. Harrods bag, tissue paper, little tag (wrapped by shop assistants, at a guess). Lily uncoiled enough to accept it, and murmur thank you.

'Aren't you going to open it, then?' said Jim, in a Father Christmas voice. Lily looked at him for the first time. He flushed. With his face so determined and his voice so fake I considered sympathizing with him, but decided against.

He has a wife for Christ's sake! They can have their own damn child!

Lily pulled at the tissue paper.

'Here, let me help,' said Jim, suddenly standing and coming round the table. Lily pulled the package away from him. He sat down, squashed. So small, and yet so effective when it comes to squashing people four times their size.

It was a Polly Pocket Fairy Princess Ballroom; pink, plastic, spangly, shiny, with electric lights that worked. It had four little dolls a quarter of an inch high with fairy dresses on, and wings. It had a balloon that went up and down, with a basket you could put the dolls in. It had a dancefloor that spun round when you turned a tiny silvery knob. The whole thing closed up into a pink star-shaped handbag that you could carry with you wherever you went. It was beautiful. Lily gazed at it.

'Thank you,' Lily murmured, and climbed down between my feet to play with it on the floor.

Nora wanted more than that.

'Do you like it, Lily?' she said, calling down to between my knees.

'Yes,' came the reply. Nothing more.

Nora looked at Jim again. I touched Lily's head gently, and said, 'I'll make some tea.' They couldn't leave immediately and actually I didn't want them to. I wanted them to see exactly how difficult, uncomfortable and completely out of their depth this situation was. I wanted them to know in their blood that Lily was nothing to do with them; to present them with a clear view of the shining armour that encircled the two of us, protecting us and hiding us yet at the same time revealing with brilliant and brutal clarity that secrets and intimacies and love such as they could never hope to know dwelt within. I wanted them to go home crying.

Lily shuffled herself and the new toy over to be between my feet at the cooker as I poured the water into the teapot. 'Move back, love, it's hot,' I said, but she shook her head. I moved the teapot to the very back of the work surface. I will not be faulted.

After shuffling back with me to the table, not looking up, she jumped up and whispered to me that she wanted to show the ballroom to the teddies, and ran upstairs.

'She seems a very affectionate little girl,' offered Nora. Yes, to me. I murmured a nothing.

Jim's face was set again. He too had prepared, and had had no idea what would happen.

'Love's not automatic, you know,' I said suddenly. 'It's not like eyes meeting across a crowded room. You have to earn a child's love.' I stopped just as I realized that my words might come over as a comfort, rather than a gibe.

Nora took them as comfort.

'I'm sure we will earn it. Won't we, darling?'

Won't we, darling. Won't we, darling. The mantra of the happily nuclear. I don't hate their being happy. The happiness they have is not the happiness I don't have. Anyway, I am happy. Quite. I think.

'Uh, yes, yes,' Jim said.

He wanted to see pictures of her as a baby. I pointed to one stuck in the door of a glass-fronted cupboard, then relented and handed it across to him. It showed her grinning and curly-mopped in front of a Christmas tree, a dark pixie aged about six months.

'She's so beautiful,' he said. Then, 'How's it been? Practically? Financially, if you like?'

I didn't like.

'Fine,' I said.

'You go to work and everything? Who looks after her?'

Do I have to answer these questions?

Well I decided I would. My reluctance to do anything civil was apparent enough. I wasn't going to give them actual ammunition.

'I work from home. She goes to a nursery, and spends some afternoons with a friend's children.'

'But that can't give you enough time, surely . . .'

'It does.' I work in the evenings sometimes, while she sleeps. But I'm not going to tell him that.

'But you don't have a nanny or anything . . .'

'We don't need one,' I said. 'Do you work, Nora?'

It turns out she is a travel agent. Turns out she is rather high up, actually, in travel agenting. Well, I suppose someone has to be.

Actually I am glad. Judges don't take babies away from happy homes to give them to career women.

Lily's voice came down the stairs: 'Mu-um, I need you . . .'

'Excuse me.' I went up. She wanted to go to the loo.

'Have the persons gone yet?'

'No, love.'

'Can they go soon?'

'I hope so.'

'I hope so back,' she said. I smiled. 'I love you,' I said. 'I love you back,' she said. I wiped her bum and said, 'Do you want to come down?'

'You're not my mummy but you are my mummy,' she said.

'That's right, honey. Janie was your mummy but she died so I'm being your mummy.'

'Who will be my mummy after you?'

'I'll always be your mummy if you want me,' I said.

'I want you,' she said.

'I want you back,' I said.

'Do they know my mummy?'

'They did, when she was alive. Well, the man did. The woman is his wife.'

'The lady.'

'Yes.'

'She's not my mummy.'

'No.'

'Children have daddies,' she said.

Not now. Why now? How does she *know?*

'Yes, love.'

'I haven't got a mummy or a daddy.'

I hugged her. 'You've got me and Grandma and Grandpa and Brigid . . .'

'And Caitlin and Michael and Anthony and Christopher and Maireadh and Aisling and Reuben and Zeinab and Larry and Hassan and Omar and Younus and Natasha and Kinsey and Anna and . . .' She was off on the game of listing the ones she loved. Reassuring herself.

'And I love mummy even if she is dead.'

'Of course. And so do I.'

'And so do I.'

'And so do you.'

'And so do you. And she loves me too.'

'Yes she does.'

'And when she comes back to life she can come and live with us.'

'She won't come back to life, darling.'

'But if she does.'

'Yes, if she does. But she won't.'

'So I'll live with you for ever and ever.'

What do you say?

'Mummy?'

'Yes, hon?'

'If you have a baby in your tummy will it have a daddy?'

Oh, blimey. Maireadh's pregnant and so's one of the teachers, so it was bound to come out at some stage.

'Yes, love. But I haven't got a baby in my tummy.'

'Can I borrow its daddy? If I want one?'

'Do you want one?'

'Yes.'

We went downstairs. Jim tried to play with the ballroom with Lily but he didn't have a clue. Anyway his fingers were too big. After another fifteen minutes or so they left. The tea was cold, untouched. Like Nora, I thought, irrelevantly. Though presumably she wasn't untouched.

*

If he wants regular visiting rights it will be very hard for me to get a court to refuse him. No one will accept now that he was violent. Nobody ever proved anything. He hasn't been, to my knowledge, since Janie's death. I could try to find out. Funnily enough, Harry might know. Harry always hated him. He *might* know. If there's anything to know. Perhaps there is.

If he wants parental responsibility he will have to apply for it. Because they weren't married, he has no claim on anything unless Janie or the courts give it to him. And she's not going to, is she?

I have parental responsibility jointly with Mum and Dad. I have three years of looking after her. I have something he doesn't have.

I don't think I frightened them off for good. Each of them, separately, seemed to have something in them that meant they would cling on. The tidiness of her clothes and her dark head hummed with efficiency, achievement, the chosen object in the correct place, priorities listed, and carefully polished successes ticked off. She wouldn't go for what she couldn't get. But she doesn't know everything. She doesn't know children. Perhaps she is beginning to know the desire for them . . . mother-hunger. Mother-hunger would eat her alive. And those who are astounded by the force of mother-hunger when it hits them are not usually prepared for the force of the tidal wave that follows: the love of a child. The love of a child can destroy nations. Love for a lover is a game next to baby love.

They each had a reason. I didn't know what. But he didn't lie when he said it wasn't a whim.

But they haven't a clue. They want the child; I love the child. I am armed to the teeth with existing love.

FIVE

In the Park with Harry

The next Saturday night, Harry was there. It wasn't till I saw him, slouching against one of the big tacky-mirrored columns that surround the dancefloor, that I got a shot of the . . . conscience? doubt? fear? that I had been holding off since talking to Ben Cooper. I was there to make friends with someone I had loved, in a way, for three years, in order to spy on him, meet his cronies and report on them to the police. I was some kind of scumbag. What kind of scumbag? The kind who would do anything to protect a tiny little big-eyed kid that my only sister, deceased, left to me to take care of. How was I protecting her? By keeping on the right side of the law. However it was that the law required.

So I lurked by the bar trying to peer over the crowd to see how he looked. Pretty much the same. Same lean slouch, same long long legs, same cropped hair, same caramel skin. No no no, I can't do this. But I had to.

It's easy to happen to be next to someone in a crowd.

In fact I was a little in front of him so that he could see me, with my same lean slouch, my same long hair, my same peaches and cream skin which has so miraculously survived so many miles of motorcycling and so many late smoky nights in Levantine dives, and which still makes people who don't know me think I must be just off the boat from the Home Counties.

When the arm slid around my waist I saw for a moment every muscle and vein and scar on it, every streak of oil beneath each nail on the hard-working hand. The back of his hand that I knew so well. For a moment, feeling that arm around me, I caught my breath. Then whoops! To the performance. Turn my head, sharp with annoyance, all prepared to slap the insolent bugger. But – good lord – but surely it can't be! Good lord, Harry! But what a surprise! All this Goodness Me had to be mouthed and acted anyway because of the volume of the music. He grabbed my hand and led me back through the turmoil towards the door. His hand was hard and cool but smoother than I recalled it.

Harry was never one for small talk so I didn't have to tell him what I was doing there, which was lucky because I hadn't prepared a reason. Does this mean I have an honest heart or a stupid brain? If I am to do this I must do it well.

'How the fuck are you?' he wanted to know. And then immediately, 'Look I'm really sorry about the chair. Really really sorry, it was stupid. Really stupid. That whole thing – um – God. I'm sorry. Forgive me, yeah?'

Lily says things like that: 'Can I have some chocolate, yes?'

Steamrollers me with positivity. Forgive him? Forgive him? No, I was just going to do something for which he would have to forgive me. That's fair, isn't it, in some sick way?

'Come and dance,' he said. Does he not want to talk? Well, it's hard to talk anyway. And we were dancing, and the years rolled back. Close up, I was glad to see, he looked older. And better. Which I was not so glad to see. A little hollower in the cheek, a little craggier in the nose. The grin more muscle and less cheek. Half-way through the number he had an erection and for a split second I believed that it would be absolutely worthwhile to forget everything about reality and tomorrow and Lily and Cooper and Jim and just let Harry pull me into a dark corner. A split second.

So I said, 'Come on, let's go to the bar.'

We retired to the edge of a crowded semi-circular banquette where we couldn't talk, and I said I had to get home because of the babysitter and he said, 'Janie's kid?' and I said, 'Yes' and he said, 'God, all that . . .' and I said, 'Do you want to hear about it?' and he said, 'Yes, I do' and that was how we ended up in the Holland Park tea-room the next day, him and me and Lily, talking about 1993.

*

'I heard a bit about it,' Harry said, fingering his coffee cup. 'You know, the gist.'

The gist. I supposed that even something that huge could have a gist. Huge. Of course, it's tiny too. A tiny little domestic tragedy. Well, the days are gone when I would get upset about somebody using a word like gist. Time was nobody could say anything. That was then. Now I am . . . adjusted to it.

'What did you think?'

'I thought what a bloody mess. I don't know – I mean, I didn't know about children then.'

'Do you now?' I was suddenly struck that Harry might have children, a wife, anything. Life doesn't stand still because I'm not there to observe it. Lily doesn't know that. She was talking to the mirror the other night on her way to bed, whispering to it: 'Now, mirror, don't go away just because I'm not here.' I remembered a letter Brigid's Caitlin had had from a kid who'd moved back to Ireland. 'Dear Caitlin, I'm six now, are you any older?'

'No. But you see people, see how it matters to them. They get that look. Like you now. I . . . no. You can understand it, sort of, but you don't have to . . . anyway.'

A silence. Harry as ever was being a little gauche when it came to grown-up things. Lily was chasing pigeons. Posh people were walking about. I found myself playing my old playground game: telling the mothers from the nannies. Children out with mothers were better dressed. Mothers like to show off. Nannies do the laundry. Trotters versus Adams, Harrods versus BabyGap. In Shepherd's Bush the equivalent would be BabyGap versus the Market. So near and yet so far. I like it up here, the posh side of the roundabout. The people may be no happier but their sad faces have better make-up.

And it's home, too, in a way. Janie and I were born working class in Holland Park just as the neighbourhood turned posh, and just as the posh parents started sending their children to Holland Park Comprehensive in those idyllic 1960s. Janie and I became scholarship girls at posh schools. We ended up talking posh to our cockney father and talking cockney to our teachers; 'Don't say what, say pardon' at home, and 'Don't say pardon, say what' at school. We were inverted snobs with no blood or breeding. At the time it was great, shoplifting in Biba and smoking joints in the park and running round with dukes' daughters, doing the ouija board in great empty flats in Eaton Square, where the nanny was too busy shagging the butler to notice what we were doing to the drinks cabinet.

Later on, I called it socialism and urban reality and thought it was great. Janie called it a mess and blamed the parents. Janie said it was a bloody fantasy and they should have made up their minds what they wanted us to be. I said surely that was our job. Janie said that they were meant to *equip* us, at least. I said, well, they equipped me . . . anyway, what more do you want? They're still married and you've got your bloody degree, for God's sake. You didn't starve or get sent down a mine. Janie said, yes, well, that's all just dandy, isn't it.

Janie always wanted to know where she stood. I wanted to make it up as I went along. Perhaps because all along I actually did know where I stood. On my own two feet – perhaps because I was earning so early – while Janie was more often standing on other people's. Come to think of it, Janie's was a more dangerous position. Janie was an attention girl. Every night till we left home, in our shared bedroom, there was either a big sisterlove or a furious sisterhate going on. And there were a million phone calls through our carefully separate universities – Oxford for her, Cambridge for me, only the best, you know, all those scholarships paid off – and the flat carefully not shared when we came back to London. But equally carefully not far apart.

I was in Clerkenwell in my grotty squat, as I reverted to what I liked to think of as my working-class roots – in fact it was just a grotesque form of insecurity: if I didn't try, I couldn't fail, could I? Apart from the dancing, I didn't know what I was good at. And the dancing didn't count. Not with my education. I stopped doing it for a while, thinking that might force me into a proper consideration of what I was 'meant' to be doing. All that happened was that I had no money.

Janie was in Camden with her baby banker boyfriend and her aspirations to worldly success. She always had crap taste in men, after Colin, the childhood-sweetheart-who-let-her-down. 'Can you blame me?' she said. 'After what Colin did, how could I ever trust a nice guy again?' Indisputable Janie logic, issued through her angelic pink mouth, corroborated by her big innocent eyes.

Harry was watching me. Harry, who has always been pure Shepherd's Bush, was looking considerably more Holland Park now. For someone who was such a post-punk anarchist urban biker squatter ten years ago, he had clearly done all right. Most of them look just the same at thirty-five as they did at twenty-five: grimy, skinny, resentful, poor, drunk, drugged, wild. But what is charmingly rebellious and sexy at twenty-five becomes an inescapable, ugly rut at thirty-five. Then at forty they die.

Harry did not look as if he were going to die. He was still wearing black pegleg jeans and a leather jacket, and no doubt the tattoos were still there underneath them, but he clearly had access to hot water, and used it, and I didn't think he'd found the jeans in a skip. Suddenly I was in 1986, lurching and pulling a skip-salvaged bathtub down the road with Harry, delighted because now we could plumb it in and I could have hot baths in my own house. Well, my own squat.

This musing was not going to bring Harry back into my confidence.

'You've a fly in your hair,' he said, reaching over to remove it. 'Or something.' Or nothing, I think.

'Lay off, Harry,' I said.

'No, you're looking good. Doing well. It's good.' He was smiling at me. Oh, Harry. Oh, really.

If this were all happening by God's own honest-to-goodness chance would I respond to this stuff? Lord knows, squabbling with Neil is no substitute for emotional satisfaction. I smiled prettily. The question that had bothered me since 1988 burned in my throat now he was here in front of me. Harry, why did you go so mad that night?

But I was here to chum up, not to sort out old tragedies. If we started sorting out, we might end up actually making friends again, and that was the last thing I wanted. Or not, I wondered, looking at his face. There is something so lovely about a face you know well.

Stop it. You were here to chum up, for Ben Cooper, for Lily, that's all.

'Do you remember the day we went to Brighton?' I said. It was the Pontiac's last outing, not that I was going to mention that yet.

'Yeah.'

'What did we do? I can't remember.' I couldn't, actually.

'Saw Janie, I should think,' he said. Suddenly I could remember. Janie was living there. She'd been incredibly bad-tempered when we left, standing on the area steps of her basement flat, complaining about where he'd parked the car.

'Why didn't you come to her funeral?' I asked, suddenly and viciously, the only thing I had said to him so far that I actually meant. Why hadn't he?

'I didn't know if I'd be welcome.'

'Oh, crap, that's why people die, so that other people can make up at funerals. You should have come. All sorts of people came.'

*

Mum and Dad, looking irrelevant, like they didn't understand and nothing understood them. Neil, trying to hold my arm. Ben Cooper was there, well wouldn't he be, his collar turned up against the grey wind under the trees out by the grave. People I didn't know.

I looked at Mum and couldn't understand how she could just be there. She gave birth to us. She should have spontaneously combusted, or dissolved, or spun away up like a tornado into a vortex of anti-matter. The child shouldn't die before the mother. It's against natural law. How can the mother just stand there? I think she felt it too.

The vicar said all sorts of nonsense and no one cried. I didn't know why I wasn't dead. We'd always been together. How could she be dead without me? We didn't bring Lily, and Jim glared at me as if he knew I had her secreted about my person, as if I was a shoplifter and he, store detective, just knew she was there in my deep deep pockets. And so in a way she was. A batch of girls we'd been at school with came, for some reason. Zeinab came and stood just behind me all afternoon, muttering in Arabic. Blessings and prayers, I think . . .

Everyone came back to mine afterwards – God, London is a terrible city, a twelve-mile drive to the nearest burial ground with room for her, and twelve miles back for the drink. We knew she was dying but were we allowed to bring her home from the hospital to die? No. Then she's taken off and sliced up and post mortemed and are we allowed to lay her out at home for the final respects? No. Mum was upset. Where's home anyway, when no one knows the vicar? Mum and Dad came in from Enfield. What the hell are they doing living in Enfield? Where the hell is Enfield?

'We can't afford to stay here any more,' they'd said, packing up in their sixties, God help us, to move their generations of living in Ladbroke Grove out to the far east. They were throwing things away. I said, 'Take all that with you. That's for Janie and me to throw away when you're dead. Don't you throw it away.' And then Mum got this sad old look in her eyes and said, 'Angie, love,' meaning, 'You're strange, *why* do you have to be like that?' like she's been saying ever since I dug up the school alligator a year after it had died to see what its skeleton looked like. She thought it was strange of me to remember so long, let alone to want to see the skeleton.

Mum's a bit deaf because she was cleaning her ear with a Q-tip coming downstairs and she fell and punctured her eardrum. Now why was she cleaning her ears coming downstairs? Neat, worriable her of all people? Perhaps everybody does incredibly out-of-character things when there's no one there to see them. Perhaps character is only what other people see; defined by being observed. Bless you, Mum, and I won't dig up Janie, don't worry. I know what her skeleton looks like because I looked at her X-rays after the crash when they thought she might survive even though she was still unconscious, and thought about how we would have laughed about it, but the laughter made my broken ribs flex and so I stopped. My broken ribs, her crushed organs. Lily, you miracle.

*

'I would have come,' he said, and I knew he was lying but I didn't know why. I was glad he was being a pig, it made it easier. Easier to betray him, but not easier to get on with him. I needed something . . . some excuse to hold us together for the duration. And not sex.

'Harry,' I said, 'can you find me a car?'

'Is a bear a Catholic?' he responded with his cheeky-chappie grin. 'Name it, Angel, and it's yours. How much do you want to spend?'

Well, of course, I didn't want to spend anything. Yes, I know I already had a car – a poor thing, but mine own. Small, white after a rainstorm, looks like a wedge of cheese, squidged up at the back, got a stereo. Couldn't remember the make. Cars have never got me, despite all Harry's blandishments on their behalf in the old days. Too many wheels.

Meanwhile, I was thinking. What I was thinking was, 'Keep it simple.'

'Well, I've got this . . . um . . . this little white thing, and it's OK, but it's got negative kudos, really, and it's ugly, and . . .' Inspiration. Go for sympathy, '. . . and if I'm never going to ride a bike again I need a car with a bit more going for it.'

'Never going to ride again?' His concern looked genuine. It was the sort of thing he could understand. 'But your leg's not that bad, is it? What's the problem?'

'Combination,' I said. I tried to look a little pathetic, a brave strong butterfly fluttering gamely against the tempests of a remorseless world; proud girl brought down but not letting it get to her, former belly-dancer-on-a-Harley taking the bus to the creche. 'I can't afford both. I need the car for Lily, for work. My leg . . . you know when you realize you're mortal?' I asked, and looked at him straight.

'Yes and no,' he said warily.

'If I did anything more to my leg now I couldn't work

at all. Not at what I do. Even now, without full use of it, I don't know how safe I'd be on a bike. I've got to work, I've got to be in good nick, because Lily needs me. I can't do things, because of what might happen. A bit different to how I was, eh? And I . . .' I didn't say that I'm never ever ever going to damage another person ever again.

'See what you mean,' he said. He was stirring his coffee. 'So. Do people think you're an old bore now? Not want to play with you any more?'

'I don't care,' I said. 'Things are different. Different priorities, different interests . . .'

Lily tired of the pigeons. 'I want juice,' she said. We slipped into the ritual.

'What do you say?'

'Apple juice,' she said.

'No,' I said. She looked as if she were about to whine. Not in front of Harry you don't. I am the perfect mother. The perfect not-mother. 'Come on, love, how do you put it if you want something?'

She looked at him, looked at me. Wise eyes.

'Darling beautiful Angeline, please please please may I have some apple juice?' she said. Oh, wow. 'May I', no less. None of your 'can I'. A simple please would have done me.

I tried not to laugh and said, 'Of course, darling.'

Harry may have developed some understanding of how it is when you have a child, but he went off into a blank during this interchange, as the child-ignorant always do. And then carried on regardless with what he was in the middle of, not taking on board that I was now committed to doing something else for someone else, and in the near future.

'So yes,' he said. 'I'm not surprised. Look at you. No bike, gammy leg, no more flowing chiffon and sequins, bed by ten, babysitters, single mother, burden on society, working all the time you're not mopping up sick . . .'

'Three-year-olds aren't sick,' I retorted. 'And I'm not a burden on society.' Of course he was teasing. Damn. Close enough to my fears that I fell for it.

'What are you doing then, if you're not wriggling?'

'Angelmum,' Lily murmured. (That's the sort of thing she calls me. All sorts of combinations of what I am, and what I am to her.)

'I am a consultant wriggler,' I said, patting her. 'I am actually something of a scholastic expert on wriggling, the art and history of it. I wrote a book on wriggling. I have designed wriggling costumes for very rich foreigners – well, for their wrigglers, not for them personally. I tell film designers how to get their harem scenes right. I do all right, thank you.' I made light and bright. I regretted my slip into defensive snappiness. Show him no weakness.

'Good for you,' he said. 'I knew you would. You always have the energy.' God bless him. 'Got a boyfriend then?' Damn him.

'Admirers,' I said, with a pretty smile. Pretty, and subject closing. 'I must get Lily her juice.'

No, I don't have a boyfriend. Not that I wouldn't like one. I'm old-fashioned that way. I like sex (as far as I can recall) and love and company, and it's nice having someone around to blame for everything. But there is a single-mother problem. It's not that men don't ask us out. They do. Men over thirty love single mothers because they feel let off the hook; we already have a kid so we're not going to start all that 'marry me marry me' biological clock stuff. Men who never grew up adore us. They think we won't notice another three-year-old round the house, won't mind whining and can't tell that the laundry load was suddenly doubled. The only person I ever met who insisted that men won't go out with single mothers was a man who wanted to lower my self-esteem so far that I would consider going out with him.

But a single mother builds up a world, a careful world. It works by balancing, by constant care. You can't jeopardize it. You can't let just anybody into it. There's a Turkish word: *enderun*. The inside world, where you live, the area you protect. Your territory. A single mother can't cry for a week if her heart is broken. You can't stay up all night if you have to work and be sweet with the infant the next day. You can't kick the child who is used to sleeping in your bed out of it for the sake of a quick thrill. You can't get your quick thrill elsewhere unless you have a particularly accommodating babysitter. You can't do anything in private. You may be able to face a child saying, 'Is he my new daddy then?', but I can't. The stakes are higher and it's not just you at stake. (Do you want a daddy? Yes.)

'You should give yourself a break,' says Brigid, who manages to be far more relaxed about these things than I am.

Brigid runs a string of admirers and half the time one of them is babysitting while she's out with another. But Brigid is tougher than me. And her kids are more interested in each other than in her sex-life. I suppose it's just that having killed Lily's mother there's nothing I would consider too great a sacrifice in the interests of her security and well-being.

'That's a bit warped, actually,' says Brigid. 'And anyway, a kid needs a dad.' Exactly, that too. If I could cut straight to being three years into true love and happily domestic ever after, then I would. And of course that would look good when I go for adoption too. But the early hit and miss stages . . . No. No, I don't have a boyfriend.

'And how about you?' I said, when I came back.

'Oh, hundreds of 'em,' he said.

'What? – Oh, no, I meant – you know, life. What are you doing?'

'I'm in the motor trade, darling, same as I always was,' he replied. 'Only better. Period cars for the movies, customized cars for the foolishly rich, gorgeous cars for weddings and bar mitzvahs, for sale or hire, whatever they want. You should come down to the showroom.'

'I'd love to,' I said. Step one accomplished. 'But, God, I probably couldn't afford anything you've got.'

'I'll find you something,' he said. 'Leave it to me. I'll have a think. I know what you want.'

Well, thank God you don't, I thought.

Lily slurped through her straw.

'Is Harry handsome?' she said.

SIX

Harry in His Showroom

Lily and I got home on Monday to find Brigid in the kitchen saying could she leave Caitlin for half an hour, and a letter in the second post from a law firm whose name I didn't recognize. I parked the girls with a magic colouring book and a glass of water, and studied the letter.

It was straightforward enough. 'As the child's father, Mr Guest wants his daughter to be with him, and is accordingly applying for a residence order under Section 8 of the Children Act 1989 . . .'

Well, I'd been expecting it. I wasn't going to ring Mum and Dad. I'd talk to them later, if I had to. Perhaps there was a simple way through this, without upsetting them. What I needed was some facts and some law.

Oh dear.

Lily and Caitlin began to squabble over the paintbrushes. I patted them absently.

I'd have to talk to Neil. I didn't want him clambering

well-meaningly through my hair if I was juggling Jim and Harry and Ben Cooper already, but I had no choice really. I knew I'd need help. Last time, when my parents and I each got parental responsibility, it was easy, because nobody was contesting anything.

Parental responsibility.

Neil might well still be angry with me, but he would help. I just didn't want to talk to him, that was all.

Brigid was late picking Caitlin up so I made tea for both of them and put them in the bath, Caitlin so red and bouncing and Lily so creamy with her long long hair. Lily was calling me Mummy. I don't always correct her. By her logic all kids have mothers, and mothers aren't dead, they're the ones that feed you and pick you up from playschool. Peter Scott hatched some cygnets once whose mother had died; when they popped out of the eggs the first thing they saw was his Wellington boots. And at regular intervals the Wellingtons would arrive and give them food. They loved the Wellington boots. By Lily's logic, I am her mother.

*

The next day I worked. An Arab airline wanted an article on the history of belly dancing for its in-flight magazine. It would probably be an excuse for lots of pictures of half-naked babes, but there we go. Six hundred pounds is six hundred pounds, and the picture choice is their business. I would give them something academic and poetic, full of

Kutchuck Hanem and Flaubert, Baladi dancing, and the fertility dances of the Mother Goddess.

I put on a video of Fifi Abdu to get me in the mood. God, that woman's hips. Even at my youngest and lithest I never ever came near her. And I was good, you know. I learnt rakkase from the gypsies of Sulukule in Istanbul, I learnt from the Ouled Nail and the Chikhat. I danced on tables up and down Charlotte Street and never once put my jewelled toe in a plate of mezes. Unless you count the time when I kicked a dish of houmous into the face of a guy who had just suggested that I 'dance on this, baby', and made to unbutton his fly.

He kept laughing, so I did my rose-water trick. I learnt it from an Egyptian dancer in Cairo, who said she always did it to French tourists in revenge for Napoleon. She did it to me – I didn't know whether to be flattered or what.

A group of us were in her sitting room, hanging out, watching dance videos, drinking tea. I danced for them, and they danced for me, and half-way through her dance she picked up a tiny glass of rose-water and carefully, delicately, put it to her mouth so that she was holding it between her two rows of teeth. Then she really danced: flinging her hips this way and that, rotating, grinding, rippling, isolating, really a very energetic dance. And her head? Motionless. She spilt not a drop. Excellent control. Then as she finished she flicked the glass with her tongue so that the liquid seemed to pour down her throat, and let the glass drop CRASH to the floor. She looked me straight in the eye, and then laughed as she sprayed the rose-water out in my face. The other women watching began the *zagareet*, the ululating cry of joy that used to terrify me before I realized it was complimentary.

Was I shocked? Yes, I was. I made her teach me. She told me about the dancers at the Casino Opera in Cairo in the 1920s, who would dance with golden candelabra on their heads, all the candles lit. 'Not so different from the poor people carrying their waterpots on their heads,' she said. 'Watch any Bedouin woman walk.' And about the girls who could hold two wine glasses on their bellies, one full and one empty, and empty the wine from one into the other, just by contracting their muscles. I saw a girl do it once, at Sahara City, a cabaret in a tent at Giza, just by the pyramids. Most things I saw I tried to learn; that one I passed by.

I did the rose-water trick to Houmous-face. He was outraged, and left. Even now, I don't know if I perhaps did something unforgivable then – like before I realized that I must not let the soles of my shoes show . . .

I got into an argument with an Egyptian about it that same night. He could not conceive that a blonde could do it, physically or culturally. I was used to that from my travels, when people often couldn't actually believe that I knew their dance at all, so I used my usual line: that the Egyptian word for dancer, *ghaziya*, comes from the root meaning outsider, foreigner, invader. I pointed out that the Turkish, *cengi*, comes from the same root as *cingene*, gypsy. Outsiders all. As he seemed interested, I tried out on him the theory that belly dancing was the current manifestation of ancient female religious dancing, which thrived among those people (outsiders, gypsies) who escaped the restrictions of the new male religions – Islam, Christianity, Judaism. It was squeezed out of proper society, yet necessary to it – that sort of thing. Why else, I asked him, did Egyptians always have dancing girls – whores, effectively, girls who would never otherwise be welcome in a respectable house – at weddings? Because, he said, stealing my thunder and my heart, their dance was originally, and in a way still is, a fertility dance, necessary to bless the union of the couple. I tried out the notion of sympathetic magic on him: that the dance imitates sex and childbirth, and in that way invites the gods to bring sex and childbirth to the happy couple. He said I was an *almeh,* not a *ghaziya* at all. That's a compliment. There was a time when women were kept so out of the world that they knew nothing of it at all, and only the *awalim* – the singers, poets and musicians – were educated. The *ghawazee* were itinerant whores, most of them. It was a class thing, a money thing, an education thing. Like most things. If you did very well, had a rich patron, and were clever, you could get to be an *almeh*.

I'm not proud. I know that I was part *almeh* and part *ghaziya*. I didn't fuck the audience and I know the history, but I danced in cafes for the money they gave me, just like innumerable women since the dawn of time who wore their fortune in their anklets and their coins sewn on to their veils. Every sequin on my tacky outfits is a homage to the Yakshi, the ancient Indian temple dancers who raised money for their goddess by dancing, by arching over backwards to allow a stranger to stick a coin to their sweaty forehead as their breasts came into view; and by shagging any passing stranger who threw a coin at them. They danced with their backs to the men; it wasn't for them, it was for the goddess. The dance would open up a channel to the divine and, by fucking the dancers, the men could make contact with it, could access the sacred force. At the same time in Cyprus, at the temple of Mylitta, girls would sell themselves to strangers, then park the money at the temple of Aphrodite until they needed it for their dowry. They were in charge of the whole thing. A good *ghaziya* could end up with a mask of little gold piastres plastered to her face, stuck with spit or sweat. And then there were the Santons – holy men in Egypt who were allowed to fuck any woman they wanted, any time, anywhere. The other women would cover the coupling with their veils. Flaubert heard of a Frenchman who pretended to be one. Or perhaps he made it up.

A respectable man will tuck his tip under your strap, without touching your flesh. A louche one will cop as much of a feel as he can get away with. I made seventy quid in tips the night I spat rose-water, sympathy money tucked into my beaded bra, plus an extra fifty from the host of Houmous-face's party, in apology. And that was a while ago.

I decided to tell the airline passengers about the time when 400 *ghawazee* were beheaded and thrown into the Nile, because they caused such unrest in the French barracks; and about how they were banished from Cairo, in 1834, threatened with fifty lashes or hard labour if they returned. The

Pashas were forever banning women, because women are *chaotic,* they won't keep their mouths shut, they promote chaos among men. Dancers are even more chaotic. They won't stay home, they intrude on male environments, disturbing the men, drawing attention to themselves and to their sexuality . . . imminent *Fitna.* Chaotic. And if there's one thing that terrifies a traditional man it is chaos.

Do you know about Flaubert and Kutchuk Hanem? Of course you don't.

Kutchuk Hanem – the Little Princess – was the mistress of the ruler Muhammad Ali's grandson, Abbas Pasha; a *ghaziya* with a protector, very lucky, very rare. She stuck around in Cairo frolicking with her sugar daddy when everyone else had been banished. But she was young then, and a fool. She took some jewellery he had given her down to the bazaar and sold it to a dealer. Now why should she do that? Why did she need the money, at her age? That jewellery should have been her pension, and she was hardly twenty. Anyway, Abbas Pasha found out, and gave her fifty lashes on his own account, for her cheek, and sent her up the Nile.

In the 1850s an American called Curtis found her. This is how she danced for him:

> The sharp surges of sound swept around the room, dashing in regular measure around her movelessness, until suddenly the whole surface of her frame quivered in measure with the music. Her hands were raised, clapping the castanets, and she slowly turned upon

herself, her right leg the pivot, marvellously convulsing all the muscles of her body. She advanced slowly, all the muscles jerking in time to the music. The rest was most voluptuous motion – not the lithe wooing of languid passion, but the soul of passion starting through every sense, and quivering in every limb. It was the very intensity of motion, concentrated and constant . . . Suddenly stooping, still muscularly moving, Kutchuk fell upon her knees and writhed, with body, arms and head upon the floor, still in measure – still clanking the castanets, and arose in the same manner . . . still she retreated, until the constantly down-slipping shawl seemed only just clinging to her hips and making the same circuit upon herself, and after this violent and extravagant exertion was marbly cold.

Words don't work. I've tried to re-create routines from written descriptions, even to do what I've been told, but unless you see it and feel it you cannot do it. That is the single reason why I took to it so when I was sixteen. I wanted something in which my body was in charge and my brain was utterly irrelevant. Sex can do it sometimes, and Janie told me pregnancy did it too. Sod off brain, you can just stop thinking and analysing for a bit, because all the blood and energy is going elsewhere, thank you.

Flaubert did manage to describe the effect of it in his description of Salome in *Herodias*:

> She twisted from side to side like a flower shaken by the wind. The jewels in her ears sung in the air, the silk on her back shimmered in the light, and invisible sparks shot out from her arms, her feet and her clothes, setting the men on fire. A harp sang out, and the crowd answered it with cheers. Without bending her knees, she opened her legs and leant over so low that her chin touched the floor. And the nomads, hardened to abstinence, the Roman soldiers adept at debauchery, the greedy publicans and the old priest soured by controversy all sat with their nostrils distended, quivering with desire.

Flaubert spent a night with Kutchuk Hanem at Esna in 1850: 'Such a night as one seldom spends in a lifetime, and I enjoyed it to the full.' He recorded her as an ornithologist might: the blue tassels of her tarboosh spread against her shoulder like a fan; the patch of decay on one of her teeth; the contractions of her hands and thighs while she slept; the singular blend of smells around her; her own dripping sandalwood oil and the nauseating aroma of bedbugs.

Awake, she fucked him and his companions, then sent away the boatmen, covered the eyes of her musicians and danced for him; a mythical dance, a lost dance: the Bee. The Queen of Sheba tempted St Anthony with it. It's a simple idea: a bee has entered into your clothing, you squeal, and wriggle, and divest yourself waft by waft of your garments until you're naked, surprised, vulnerable, standing on your beautiful carpet, in your cabin, on your boat, on the Nile, at sunset, with your musicians blindfolded and a white man, the great author, besotted at your feet.

She had nothing but contempt for the westerners who wanted her to dance naked. She wore scarlet nipple caps beneath her gauze tunic for Abbas Pasha, but in the main, since then, she had been careless, lazy, self-possessed. She didn't care that Nubian Aziza said that she didn't know how to dance. She didn't care when Flaubert's man Joseph said he had seen the Bee danced better by a man. She didn't care that boys impersonated her; that trained monkeys imitated her dances at the *mouled*, the saints' festivals. She's been mocked worse than any of them could ever hope to now.

She slept with her head on Flaubert's arm, and before dawn rose to huddle over her brazier for an hour. 'How flattering it would be,' he wrote, 'to one's pride, if at the moment of leaving you were sure that you left a memory behind, that she would think of you more than of the others who have been there, that you would remain in her heart.' God, how easy a romantic finds it to love out of context, out of place, with a mid-nineteenth-century American Express card and a return ticket. It's somewhere else, it doesn't count. She's foreign, it doesn't count. She's a whore, it doesn't count. She's different, it doesn't count. It's not far to she's female, it doesn't count. And that justification is still alive and breathing.

His mistress Louise Colet travelled that way in 1864. She wrote that Kutchuk Hanem was 'still living – a living mummy'. There's no point being jealous of the exotic, any more than of the dead.

The phone went, but I was way up the Nile and didn't answer it. Ben Cooper's voice came over the answering machine. 'Hope you're out being sociable, Angie!' he said cheerfully. 'Speak to you soon, OK? Byee!' For all he sounded like a holiday rep, the message was clear.

I shook off my oriental miasma and rang Harry. Would he be around tomorrow at the showroom because I was going to be in the neighbourhood. How convenient! It was easy actually: Zeinab lives round the corner and I needed to see her anyway to go over some designs. It didn't seem odd to be covering myself. When I was a child I used to raid the fridge and wonder whether cold chickens carried fingerprints, and what my mother would do when she found out that it was I who had had the piece of drumstick. Janie and I thought we might have identical fingerprints because we looked a lot like each other. People who didn't know us well sometimes mistook us for each other. When we were small we wished we were twins because we longed to play tricks.

*

I had a dream that night. I was dancing in my green and gold, one of my first costumes. I was on the floor, arching back and giving the little Turkish cymbals a fair rattling with my arms undulating way up above my head. I was an arc, my arms and hair reaching almost to the floor, almost into a crab, perfectly balanced, a semi-circle of moving shimmering green and gold light, tinkling. Then I was on the table (I never do that move on the table, my hair is too long, it goes in the food). Then I was surrounded by flame, a ring of fire and beyond it a ring of faces, flushed and having fun. Then I rose into the air like a piece of burning paper, floating up and up, as light as light. And then I woke up.

I've dreamt it before and I will again. I knew what it was about. One night a man had poured a bottle of brandy on the table while I was dancing and had set fire to it. For what? To see me jump? To frighten a woman? To destroy a performance? To impress his friends?

I had hated it not just for the obvious reasons, but also because he had broken the territory. I was performing; I was dream woman, I was out of bounds. He had tried to give me a clutch of banknotes afterwards; I had refused them. He should not have even spoken to me. No one should. Ahmed and the musicians accepted, which was only fair, because we shared the tips, but then not fair at all, because it wasn't them he'd tried to incinerate. He had given five hundred pounds. He was an Englishman. I'd been surprised. He never came to the restaurant again, for which I was glad, because he was a psychopath. I think Ali banned him.

It was my basic fear and worry dream. I went in to look at my basic reassurance and comfort and found her sleeping sound and sweet. I brought her into bed with me. Well, there's never anyone else in there. She woke up to tell me she'd like a loo paper roll hanging on the wall by her bed so she didn't have to get out of bed and wake me and get me to go and get loo paper when she wanted to wipe her nose, then she fell straight back to sleep, and kicked me most of the night.

*

Harry's showroom was in the back-of-beyond beyond Ealing, but God it was flash. Expanses of window, gigantic yucca plants and bijou little open-plan office area, and acres of indoor parking. He showed me his catalogue of bikers: fat Harleys with fat riders, available for Hell's Angels movies and building society adverts, browse through and pick the ones you like. He had at least forty cars, mostly American but with a little gaggle of 1950s and '60s English cars in a corner: Anglias and Morris Minors and the mock-Tudor ones.

I had a sudden flashback to my parents' street off Ladbroke Grove when I was small: the butcher, the greengrocer, the electrics shop, the sweetshop (sherbet lemons and Lucky Bags), the post office, the off-licence, the hairdresser with the Marcel-waved plaster heads in the window, gold hair and mauve eyeshadow; the chemist with the gloopy fat green and red bottles, where a dragon lived, or so my dad told me; and the baker that we never went to where the cat sat on the doughnuts in the window, and once I saw the Hungarian lady who ran it wiping some oozing cream off a cake and licking her finger. But that's not why we didn't go there. We didn't go there because once they accused Janie of nicking a bar of chocolate. Which she didn't. I know because I was there. My five-year-old fury at the injustice to my innocent younger sister was ballistic.

That street now has two estate agents (short-term company lets and service flats), a car hire, three kebab shops, three late-night grocery stores (one Lebanese, one Turkish and one Pakistani), a Swedish cafe. Only the post office and the offie remain. Oh and the Greek restaurant, which was always there, run by Costas who we were at primary school with, and with whom my Dad over the years has discussed all these bloody newcomers spoiling the neighbourhood. Costas has a turquoise Rolls-Royce now. The cars on the street back then were now the ones in Harry's showroom.

'They take me right back,' I said to him, stroking the sweet little chrome lid on an Anglia's headlamp.

'Well here's one that will,' he said, and led me round the back of the American section where lounged, in all its louche glory, my Pontiac. It looked nice: gleaming dark madonna blue, cream leatherette, chrome that looked loved. In the days when it had lived outside my squat in Clerkenwell it had had mould growing on its whitewall tyres, icicles inside in winter and in summer nasty little insects breeding in its rotted upholstery. I had used it for storage in the end: my bike tools had lived under the hood where the engine had been. Someone had done a lot of work on it. It was not difficult for me to gasp convincingly.

'Is that my car!' I whooped.

Harry misunderstood me. 'Um, no – I mean . . . it's not the one I had in mind for . . .

'No, no, I didn't mean that. I mean, is that the old crock that lived on my doorstep? I thought it got squashed – ' Damn. I hadn't meant to mention that. I covered quickly. 'God, isn't it lovely. Do you know, I saw one just like this – well, there can't be another one like this, must have been this one. It was only a few weeks ago, in South Ken somewhere, that's right, I was trying to park in Pelham Crescent, I was going shopping . . .' I burbled on.

'Very likely, I use it as my runabout,' he said, but nothing more. Perhaps I shouldn't lead. A telephone warbled and Harry fished it out of his pocket. Oh Lord, Harry was a yuppy, ten years after everyone else. Well, good for him.

'Yeah, hi . . . mm . . . what, now? . . . no it's just I've got someone with me . . . no, just an old girlfriend . . . well excuse *me* . . . yeah . . . OK . . .' He covered the receiver and said to me, 'Got to go and meet my boss – come along and then we'll go and get lunch.' But of course. Just an old girlfriend indeed. He winked at me while being talked to. 'OK. Half an hour,' he said.

We went in the Pontiac. Vrroom vroom, and comfortable. 'Do you remember,' we both started at the same time. 'You go,' he said.

'Trying to work out mathematically whether the likelihood of arguments due to the penury caused by the expense of running an eighteen-miles-to-the-gallon motor was adequately compensated for by personal space guaranteed by the width of the front seat in the case of such argument erupting?' I said.

'I remember you half a mile away from me over by the door sulking, that's for sure.'

Then I remembered very clearly lying almost full-length on my front along that seat trying to give him a blowjob while he was driving, and him having to pull over not out of overwhelming desire but because he was laughing so much, and . . .

He was giving me a sideways look as we came round Shepherd's Bush roundabout. 'Yes, I remember that too,' he said.

I hadn't slept with a man since before the accident, the death, the birth. I don't know why. A thousand reasons, each one good enough but no reason at all. Harry knew me. Harry had always known me. Perhaps it would be best under the circumstances not to think about what Harry had always known, and always known how to do. Specially with that look on his face.

'Why haven't we got the roof down?' I demanded suddenly.

'Do you want it down?' he said. 'I thought you wouldn't have.' He doesn't know me at all. Phew. 'Girls don't, mostly. They say it spoils their hair.'

'You've been with the wrong kind of girl, Harry.' It popped out before I could stop it. So much for trying to change the subject.

'Come on,' I said, 'pull in and we'll do it now.'

He started laughing. So did I.

'No no no,' I said. 'Stop it. Stop it.'

'I didn't start it,' he said, pulling in to the kerb, 'but if you like . . .' and he lunged towards me. He was half mocking, but if I had liked . . . I jumped out of the car and started fiddling with levers under the roof. But the roof was completely new; it didn't work the way the old one had (not that 'work' was quite what the old one had ever done).

'Here, let me,' he said. 'Angeline and Harry by the side of the road, trying to get a vehicle to do something. Timeless, isn't it.'

'Where are we going, anyway?' I said.

'To South Ken, to see Eddie.'

'Should have gone down by Earl's Court,' I said. Eddie, I thought. Already. Steady. Oh, for God's sake.

OK, good. Going to see Eddie. That's what we wanted, that's good. A little sooner than expected, but – no, it's good. Harry's partner. Criminal. Harry is a criminal. Shit.

He might not be. Oh, please. A man's partner is a criminal, a man is a criminal. I don't even know what kind of criminal Eddie is. I know nothing. I'm going to a criminal's house with a criminal in a criminal car and . . . What kind of criminals are they? Well they're not burglars, are they. Not muggers. Gangsters, I suppose. Drugs, probably. Vice. Stolen goods. Bank robbers. Fraud. Forgers. Pelham Crescent! Successful, that's what kind.

Actually it might be worth finding out.

I have no idea what I am meant to do. Chum up.

Lie.

SEVEN

Eddie's House

Eddie Bates's house was only about eighteen times flasher than Harry's showroom. South Kensington is truly a salubrious area. No English people live there at all, except, evidently, Eddie. No one is rich enough.

Oh, the rising layers of Bates's white stucco, the gleam – achievable only by generations of devoted care and regular repainting – of the black railings rising from the smoothly laid York stone pavement. Oh, the clean wide stone steps leading up to the sober black door, with its polished knocker, forbidding weight, and tight little smile of a polished brass letterbox. Oh, the little round-headed bay-trees in their slatted cedar-wood jardinieres. The whole thing looked steam-cleaned. I hadn't seen anything so clean since I first saw Lily in her fishtank-cot at the hospital.

And, oh, the blank eyes of the oriental girl in an apron who admitted our grubby everyday selves.

I thought criminals were meant to be vulgar, but this

place was straight out of *Interiors.* The parquet was just so, and strewn with Persian rugs. The furniture was more Sotheby's than World of Leather. The flowers looked as if they were delivered fresh every morning from the Conran shop just across the road by a beautiful virgin dressed in white lawn woven by nuns. The air was rarefied, and the level of domestic hygiene preternatural. Curiously, it all looked like a very upmarket version of my own taste, which runs to kelims, stripped floorboards, and bunches of daffodils from the market.

'Jesus, Harry!' I exclaimed. 'You don't get this from used cars, surely.'

'Eddie's into all kinds of business,' said Harry. I bet, I thought.

'Come, please,' said the girl, and disappeared, leaving us in what I assumed to be the sitting room – no, the drawing room. I supposed the Chagall was original. And what looked like a Degas. Harry flung himself on to a *chaise-longue.* I hovered before selecting a little blue and gold damask item as the one least likely to be sullied by my quotidian bum.

'And slaves too,' I murmured, watching the girl go.

'Angeline,' said Harry reprovingly. Oh, Lord, I suppose it's bugged. I'd bug my own drawing room if I were a millionaire gangster.

And in he came. Eddie Bates. *Charming* man. Grey-haired, fine-profiled, twinkly-eyed, late fifties or so. Shakespearean actor of the old school type. Looked sort of familiar, as types do. Looked actually as if he had adopted the type by deed poll. Wonderful voice. 'Harry, m'boy', that kind of thing.

'Eddie, this is Evangeline Gower.' My full name, no less. Formal.

'Hello,' I said, jumping up, smiling, putting out my hand.

'Evangeline,' said Eddie Bates.

Now I knew why my mother had chosen it: for this moment. For Eddie Bates to say it. Nobody had ever done justice to my name before.

Charmed, he was charmed. I was charmed. How charming. Glass of sherry. Why, yes! He looked at me with as-it-were pleased astonishment. How wonderful of Harry to have produced me. Charming!

Then I was to excuse them for a moment, and they slipped off together to do whatever it was they had to do, and I was left to ponder whether the shocked look on the Chagall mermaid's face was because she disapproved of the Degas dancer showing her legs like that, and to wonder whether I was meant to follow them and listen at the keyhole.

No. But still, better things to ponder. Like . . . um . . . the layout of the house. The number of staff. The phone number. The contents of the drawers in the little bureau over in the corner. The nearest exit. The distance of the drop from the window to the pavement – just in case, you know.

I opened one drawer of the bureau, heart spinning. A duster. And another. A little black gun lay snugly on a velvet scarf. I closed the drawer again and wiped the handle with my sleeve. Felt sick. Maybe he has invisible security cameras to match the bugs. Maybe that's why the mermaid is looking at me funnily. If I go to find a bathroom to throw up they'll think I'm snooping. I am snooping. I bolted the sherry and sat down.

The maid slipped back in to the room.

'Oh, is there a bathroom I could use?' I said brightly.

She looked a query with her eyebrows.

'Bathroom,' I said. 'Lavatory. Loo. Cloakroom. Powder room? Where you keep the euphemisms?' I hoped he had more articulate staff for when he gave parties. 'Toilet?' I said finally, giving up the prejudices of my education. It was evidently one of her three words.

She led me out into the hall, up a staircase that would have done Vivien Leigh proud, and chivvied me into a bathroom not much bigger than my flat, though much warmer. Here, I was glad to see, some of my prejudices were confirmed. Shag pile to wade through, and gold taps in the shape of dolphins. I was particularly pleased with the triangular bath with Jacuzzi attachments, and the fridge beside it. Locking the door, I washed the fear off my face with cold water, and felt in the loo cistern for little polythene packets of drugs. Oh, I've seen *The Sweeney*, I know what goes on. There was nothing. Nothing in the fridge, either, unless you count the champagne and the second little black gun.

'He must be expecting an emergency,' I thought, and sat on the loo. 'I suppose there's one in every room, just in case.' I wasn't reassured. I tried a minute or two of yoga breathing (close your eyes, breathe in to the count of four, hold for two, out to the count of eight, concentrate on your third eye *from within*), and a bit more cold water, then ambled downstairs again, looking out for snub black barrels poking out from behind the turn-of-the-century masterpieces on the walls. I could not see how being here increased my good character and suitability as a responsible parent staking a claim on her parental responsibility. But between my sense of the ridiculousness of the situation and the taint of fear, I found myself amused. Actually, I was enjoying it.

Harry and Eddie were waiting for me in the hall. A few 'ah, there you are's and a suggestion we stay for lunch. I murmured about Lily, picking up, that sort of thing.

'Who and what is Lily?' asked Eddie. By his demeanour, you would have thought that nothing to do with me was too minor for his attention.

I didn't want to tell him. It seemed bad luck to mention her in this house. 'My child,' I murmured, and started trying to talk about Chagall.

'Little girl! Lovely!' he expounded, before telling me that he loved children, they so brighten life, don't they, make you realize what it's all about, what it's all for. I was to get a babysitter, that's the thing isn't it, and come for dinner one day.

'In fact,' he said, looking bright-eyed, 'come tonight!' It sounded as if this were the best idea he'd ever had. 'Harry, bring this charming gel to dinner,' he said. Harry simpered, and that was it.

'And how much did he pay for *you*,' I murmured to Harry on the doorstep.

'More than you could possibly imagine in your wildest dreams!' he grinned. 'And he's not paid it off yet.'

'Jesus, Harry, what is that guy?' I felt it only realistic to be frank. 'And what is he to you?'

'He's a very successful businessman, who set me up financially to set up my business, from which he derives a great deal of pleasure and enough profit to make it worth his while. Sometimes I feel like his personal mechanic, but more often I just pass it off that he's my patron. He loves the cars. Borrows them whenever he wants. Doesn't have to be bothered with owning them. Can't abide to have things sitting around not earning. It's simple enough.'

We climbed into the Pontiac.

'I'll drop you off,' he said, forgetting that we were going to have lunch. 'And I'll pick you up. Can you get a babysitter? You could borrow Jean from the showroom if you want.' Oh, so you own people too? I didn't explain that a child generally likes at least to have been introduced to its babysitter. The niceties of courtesy to children seemed a little small under the circumstances. Small, but comforting. I pictured Brigid and Lily reading *Little Rabbit Foo Foo* to each other, tucked up on the sofa. It nicely negated images of little black guns.

As I stepped out of the Pontiac in Shepherds Bush I realized why Eddie had looked familiar. He was the man who had set fire to the tablecloth.

EIGHT

Dinner with Eddie

When I got in I called Cooper.

'Ah, yes,' he said non-committally. 'I'll call you back.' God knows what all that was about. I think he just liked to be mysterious. Who would he be hiding from in his own office?

He called back. I told him everything that had happened, except that I was going back that evening. I wasn't sure that I was, for one thing.

He was very pleased with developments.

'Is that it then?' I said hopefully.

'Oh, no, dear, no,' he crooned. 'No no no.' I got the message. 'Now when will you be seeing the young man again?'

'Whenever I like,' I said.

'And the older man?'

I paused. 'Well, I could, I suppose.'

'Oh, yes, you must. As soon as possible without causing

alarm. You must visit him again, I should think, don't you? And pick something up for me while you're there?' His perkiness was almost unbearable.

'You didn't say anything about that.'

'I said await further instructions, I seem to remember. So here they are. In order to help put some naughty men where they belong, just get me the diary and the address book, would you, love? Both black leather, to my belief. If you could have a look at the computer, so much the better. Any files of names and addresses. Take a spare disc or two. He uses an IBM, I assume you're literate. I'll get a couple of discs round to you, why not. And keep your ears open, and your mouth shut, and that will probably be it.'

I should have known. He's blackmailing me and there's nothing I can do about it. I'm in. I'm tarnished. If people give you shit you end up covered in it. There's nothing I can do about it.

'Why me, Ben?' I asked tiredly.

'Because you're there, Angie. It's only a little thing.'

I hate being called Angie.

*

Funnily enough it was Harry that I wanted to talk to about it all. The emotional urge came through nanoseconds before brain said, 'No, actually. Harry's a criminal, remember? He's the enemy. Remember?'

So I called Neil, to do a bit of blackmail of my own. It was all his fault. If he hadn't jumped out of the car like a self-important nincompoop I would never have . . . and none of this would have happened. And I'd only have Jim to worry about. Neil's secretary told me he was due back tomorrow.

So I rang Fergus Droyle. Fergus is a funny creature. He's been a crime reporter for a million years and he thinks he's a war correspondent. Drinks too much, keeps getting divorced, moons around regretting things all the time, mostly things he never had in the first place. Can't get over the terrible things he's seen in his life.

We met under false pretences. A curious situation exists whereby holiday companies and national tourist boards offer free holidays to newspapers and magazines, in the hope – not the understanding, mind you – that a flattering article will be the result. A women's magazine decided that one of these trips – to Algeria – would be a great way to get me to Algeria for nothing so that I could visit the Ouled Nail and write a searing reportage on how they live now; Fergus's paper decided that it would be a great way to get him to Algeria to do a bit of legwork on a drug connection he thought he had spotted. In fact we were both corralled with eight other journalists (well, six journalists, an editor's nephew and a travel editor's secretary who was owed a treat having been passed over for promotion) for a week in a luxurious hotel. We were not let out of sight, and force-fed beer and camel-rides. We had a lovely time. Fergus tried to get off with each female in the party in turn, and kept muttering, 'Fair as these foreign hills may be, they are nay so fair as hame'; I gave him some very basic Arabic lessons (everything I knew) and we drank a lot and got sunburn. It was hard to believe that I was in the same country as the one I had passed through eight years before. Well, I wasn't, I suppose. I was in third-world holiday land. It's great if you ignore absolutely everything you know about reality.

'Droyle, crime desk,' he said, importantly, as he answered the phone.

'Fergus!' I cried, pleased as ever to hear the mutter of machines and office life on the line in the background, and to know I was not part of it. All the same, you have to slip into the brusque argot, otherwise they think you have nothing to do with your time, and despise you. 'Angeline. Got two minutes?'

'For you? Don't make me laugh. Just going into conference, though. What is it?'

'Who's Eddie Bates?'

A silence.

'Why?'

Oh, damn. Why indeed. I wished I'd thought of something. So I did, quickly.

'Friend of mine's planning a deal with him.'

'Why you asking me?'

'Oh, I thought you knew him, or about him. You mentioned him to me one time. I just wanted to check what it was.'

'Did I? I doubt it.'

'Oh, well . . . but you do know him?'

'If I knew anything worth knowing about Eddie Bates, I wouldn't be doing this crap job, that's for sure. That's the whole point of him. Nobody knows.'

'But everybody must know something, otherwise they wouldn't know there was anything not to know.'

'Exactly,' he said.

'So what is it you all know? Because I don't.'

'We all know he's a villain, Ange. So you tell your friend, from me, that unless he's that way inclined himself, and presumably he's not or he'd know anyway, not to have anything to do with him.'

'What kind of villain?'

Fergus said he had to go into conference now, and if I liked he'd call me later. I said yes please, this afternoon, please.

*

Then I went and got Lily from nursery, and we watched *The Snowman* twice in a row even though it was broad sunny daylight, and ate fish fingers with mayonnaise and gherkins. Then we went round to Brigid's and said could she come over that night. Sure, she said, Maireadh was staying and she could mind Caitlin and the boys (Anthony, Michael and Christopher, three little hooligans dressed always in the most beautifully hand-knitted jumpers from all their devoted aunts in Fermoy, County Cork). Where are you going, she wanted to know. Dinner with Harry, I told her.

'Harry the old boyfriend?' she said, and started to get excited about my marriage prospects. God bless her. Whenever I start trying to fix her up – usually with Liam, who runs the snooker club on the corner where Brigid does the bar some nights – she swears blind that there's nothing a man could ever do for her beyond take her to the movies and buy her a glass of Dubonnet. That's what she drinks. Dubonnet. 'A woman needs a man like a fish needs a bicycle,' she says, which for some reason sounds hysterical in her accent, with her pictures of the Pope in every room. 'The Pope's a pishogue,' she says, 'but I've a lot of respect for pishogues.' And what the hell is a pishogue. It's a superstition.

'Harry's handsome,' said Lily.

'Is he now,' said Brigid. 'Well, so much the luckier for Angeline.'

Then we went to the park and ate ice-cream and flapjacks. Lily told me there was a boy in her school called Jack and she called him Flapjack. And that Flapjack called Jennifer Jennyfish. And if a fish went on holiday how could you tell?

Her skin is much better in the sun. Last year I could hardly bear to let her go bare-armed. You could almost see the London filth sneaking into the raw flesh. Two oily baths a day, a layer of vaseline night and morning, special coverings for pillows and mattresses, only cotton clothes, special washing powder, hoovering every day, no carpets in the flat, no artificial food, no cow's milk or food made with cow's milk, three different homoeopaths ('What was her birth like?' they ask politely for their notes. 'Any trauma at all?'), a cranial osteopath, a Chinese herbalist and an aloe vera plant, its fleshy leaves torn off, slit open and the pulp applied direct. And no idea if any of it made the slightest bit of difference.

Every night for two years she'd woken at least twice. That made 730 nights she'd slept in my bed, because when a baby is scratching herself fit to weep, and weeping, in the middle of the night, you don't leave her to do it alone. And I couldn't stand up all night. And I didn't fit in her cot. She still wakes every night at five to midnight. Regular as clockwork. If I go out I try to be in by ten to.

When I'd asked her what she wanted for her third birthday she'd said, 'Dairy products.'

How dare Jim want her.

He's her father, said a tiny voice. A child needs a father.

Not that kind of father.

Who are you to decide?

Her mother's big sister. Janie was going to leave him anyway. She was always going to leave him.

But she never did. People do things if they really want to.

She was going to leave him.

Tell that to the judge.

Jim must not know that I am seeing Harry. He knew Harry in the old days, knows his dodginess. He's dim but he's not that dim. How *does* the court find out about whether you're a good parent or not? What if they find out about all this? I've got to make an answer to the lawyers. I wish Neil were back. I hate to be dependent.

A child needs a father.

She's never asked about a father before. There are enough children in our neighbourhood who have none for it to seem normal. I always thought I'd tell her if she asks. Tell her . . . what seems right. I can't bear for her to feel unloved. But why else would he not have been here with her? 'Your father couldn't be bothered with you, darling.' Well the child has a legacy to come to terms with, we all know that. I'll just keep her safe and try to bring her up strong to deal with it when she has to. There must be a limit to how long I can get away with these amiable generalizations.

She interrupted my musings to sing the Farmer wants a Wife. Oh, and the Wife wants a Child, and the Child wants a Dog, and the Dog wants a Bone. 'Can we have a dog?' No, my darling, we can't. (You've already got a dog. A dog of a father. The Dog wants the Child.)

I have to steal a criminal's most personal documents, baby girl. He keeps a gun in every room and I have to steal his most personal documents otherwise your father will take you away and ruin you like he ruined your mother.

Should I have just accepted the drink-drive thing? I could have told them how it happened. Neil would have stood up for me. I think. In the circumstances. I might have got off.

Well. I didn't accept it.

Guns kill people, that's what they're for. That's why people have them. If I get killed your grandma will look after you. If I go to prison your grandma will look after you. Your grandma will look after you.

Oh, my God, what am I going to do.

*

I rang Fergus again when we got in. He was out of the office. I left a message. I rang him at home and left a message there too.

*

I dressed nicely for dinner. Chum up means be nice. Following instructions. Cooper must be some kind of fool to think I can do this.

'And that will probably be it,' he'd said. Do I trust him? Do I hell. He could carry on wanting things as long as he liked. I considered just failing, not even trying. What would he do? I think he would insist that I try harder. Actually I hate to think what he might do.

If I try, if I succeed, he might leave it at that. I had to try.

Looking at my fairly meagre wardrobe, I wondered what outfit would read 'dim dippy innocent ignorant girly' without reading 'dim dippy innocent ignorant sexually available girly'. I needed a self-adjusting outfit, that went from girly to swift getaway in one easy move. Flat soft shoes, trousers, nice blouse – the green silk, good, it's clean – not too much cleavage.

Why did he invite me?

Does he remember me?

Ten years on, does a psychopath remember the face of a girl he tried to set on fire?

It was such a mad thing to do. To get a thrill, to risk – what? What did he risk? Well, Ali could have called the police, I suppose. He wasn't the type to, but would Bates have known that? Ali would always avoid anything that caused ructions or questions. Mr Discreet. Obviously a little cash changing hands at the appropriate moment would be more to his taste than insurance, statements, upset customers. His place was a bit of a male haven: Levantine Lotharios out with the wrong woman, that kind of thing. Smooth it over, brush it away.

I had a sudden and very nasty paranoid delusion that Bates had paid Ali in advance for the privilege of setting me on fire. No. Ali wouldn't have done it. I'm sure he wouldn't.

Bates didn't remember me. He torched me as a dancer, a symbol, a woman in a sexual uniform playing a role. I was not me, to him. I preferred him not to remember me. It made everything easier. Less difficult, at least.

Ten minutes' yoga breathing, bit of make-up, kiss Lily good night in her bath. 'You're a smelly lipstick woman,' she said, wrinkling up her face.

Why had he invited me?

*

We ate in the dining room on the first floor, but not before we'd spent almost an hour drinking frozen vodka with the mermaid and the dancer. There were just the three of us and it was quite, quite weird. I was too nervous not to drink: I wanted to, for one, and it was obviously the point of the evening anyway. Bates was charm personified. Oozing. Little canapes, refills, cigarettes, lighter, looking into my eyes as he held the lump of malachite up to the tip of my Benson. It was a nasty moment. Flame, and his face.

'So what do you do, Evangeline?' he asked, so courteously, leaning back in his Chesterfield, once all my needs had been fulfilled.

'I'm a writer,' I said, taking the lead before Harry could say anything. 'Articles and so on.'

'How marvellous,' he purred, like Shere Khan. 'And what do you write about?'

'Art and culture, mostly,' I ad-libbed. 'I specialize rather in the Arabic and Islamic subjects. I lived in North Africa for a while, travelling about and studying. I spent some time in harems, due to lucky contacts, and I've written about that sort of thing too.'

'How fascinating. And where do you write? Anything that I might have seen?'

'Well, it's rather a specialist world, you know,' I said, praying to God that it wasn't a world he specialized in. Or knew anything at all about, actually, because there was a limit to how long I could talk if dancing was not a permitted subject. Which it wasn't. I was not going to jog his memory. Of course he might have set fire to endless women in public places, but you can't be sure. I knew he hadn't done it to any of the other belly dancers – not in London anyway. It's the sort of thing that gets around, you know.

'Not a world I know anything about,' he said, as if in answer to my prayers. Too pat? Was he trying to mislead me? Don't be paranoid. Actually, do be paranoid. 'But how marvellous, for an English woman. To be so involved in a foreign culture.'

He didn't take his eyes off me. I got the impression that he was sorry I was wearing trousers. He would have been looking at my legs, that's for sure. I smiled, like the chummy girl I was being.

'And what name do you write under,?'

'Oh, my own,' I said. 'Angeline Gower.'

'Lovely name,' he said, and we made some pathetically dull small talk about why Angeline and not Evangeline, and what names say about people, and so on and so forth. I didn't say that Eddie Bates sounded like a small-time East End crook. Harry was not contributing.

'And what's your business, Eddie?' I asked. Well, she would, that chummy girl.

'This and that, this and that. Property, mainly; some restaurants, a bit of development, investments, information technology. Harry here's motor business, as you know, is my little pet.'

He was very patronizing. Harry didn't seem to mind. It surprised me. He used to be such a feisty lad. I wondered what had happened to him over the years to change him. I wondered how they had met.

'So how did you two meet?' I asked.

'Ah, well, I knew Harry to be a reliable fellow, so when he came to me with his business proposition I decided to invest in him.'

No. That was all wrong. Harry had never been reliable. A mongoose on speed wouldn't think that Harry was reliable. And yet the business was making money. Or seemed to be. Perhaps it's money-laundering. Perhaps – and it made sense – Harry was Eddie's private tax-loss and launderette. God, Harry. Bought. And you used to be – well, not someone I would ever have imagined to be for sale.

'And I love the cars, you know. Bit of a little passion of mine really.'

Yes, yes. My mind was starting to race. The burglar alarm's little red eye was flashing at me from its eyrie up in the cornicing. I was not going to be able to leave a window open in the downstairs loo and sneak back later. I was not to waste time.

'So how long have you been in business together, then?' It's just small talk. Just small talk.

'It must be more than a year now, Harry, mustn't it?' Harry grunted an assent. He'd hardly said a thing. I wished he would.

Only a year. I had thought it had been longer. A year

isn't long to bring a business like that into profit, I wouldn't have thought.

The blank-eyed girl looked round the door.

'Come,' said Bates, with a crocodile smile. 'Let's eat.'

*

The food came up in a dumb waiter, and Bates brought the plates over to us. Noblesse oblige hung in the air like cheap scent. God, but we were meant to be honoured. Harry, thank God, perked up with the smoked fish and coriander soup, and made useful with the Pouilly Fume. The Fleurie was breathing gently in the corner: three bottles, all open. The table was laid for three. Clearly we were meant to be getting plastered.

'Have you seen the Islamic exhibition at the Royal Academy?' Bates inquired. More small talk? How long is this going to last?

'Yes, I have,' I said. 'It's *marvellous*.' Taking a leaf out of his vocabulary.

'I'm planning to go soon. Perhaps I could persuade you to go again. I'm sure your expertise would make it far more enriching for me.'

Ah.

The soup went down; the roast duck arrived.

'In fact, before you go I must take your telephone number. Harry, you don't mind, do you?' Harry smiled blandly, and almost giggled. I was beginning to hate him. 'In fact – Harry, fetch my diary, would you, it's on the desk.'

I almost flushed when he said the D word. Harry trotted off obediently. Woof woof! What kind of bone does that little dog want?

Bates drew a long slim black book out of the inner pocket of his jacket. 'Now.'

I gave him the number, and watched as the book slipped back out of reach. I'd have to fuck him to get it at this rate.

'I'd hate to embarrass our mutual friend,' he murmured, looking as if nothing would actually give him more pleasure, 'so I'll mention now that you are the most beautiful woman I have seen for a while, and your pleasure is my command. I hear you dance.'

Time stood still for a moment. I don't know if he noticed.

I took a sip from my glass. A crystal flute about a foot tall. Bad move. The vodka was beginning to tell.

'Oh, did Harry tell you that? Yes, I used to.' Loosen up. Only thing to do. 'But I had an accident. You know.' God, did he? I'd meant to follow up on the least dangerous of the things he'd just said. I had a horrible feeling I was shimmying up an even shakier branch of the conversation tree.

'Oh, dear,' he said, all concern. 'Nothing serious I hope?'

'It's just left my leg a little stiff. Dancing isn't so much fun any more.' How much had Harry told him?

He was gazing at me. 'Such beautiful hair,' he said. 'Beautiful colour.'

I'm not fucking anyone for Ben Cooper. For my safety. For Lily. I don't do that.

'I wish I'd seen you dance,' he said. 'Perhaps I can persuade you.'

Harry came back with a fat leather diary.

'So, how about next week?' said Bates. 'Wednesday or Thursday? I'm leaving the country tomorrow night, but just for a few days. I'll call you when I return. Yes?' He wrote it in his book.

'Marvellous,' I said. Duck and ashes in my mouth.

*

After the creme caramel, the coffee and the petits fours, he moved us into a smaller upstairs sitting room where brandy and cocaine awaited, nicely laid out on a tray. He put me on a sofa and told Harry to take the diary back upstairs 'and lock it in the drawer like a good fellow'. He had taken off his jacket and left it in the dining room. One out of two ain't bad. I'd have to go to the loo. As I rose to do so he took my arm, took my waist, stared at what was visible of my cleavage and then put his face very close to mine.

'You're not still attached to him, are you?' he said.

Oh, no. Not at all.

'Good,' he said. 'I do look forward to seeing you next week.'

'So do I,' I lied.

Harry came back. I went to the loo, via the dining room where I lifted the address book from his jacket pocket and stuffed it down the back of my trousers. I was aware that this was a very stupid thing to do, and I truly believed that I had no choice.

Pray he doesn't grab my waist again.

I was safe. As if he had realized that he wasn't going to be fucking me then and there, he seemed suddenly bored with the whole thing. Eddie had a line of coke; Harry declined – actually he had hardly drunk anything either – and so did I.

Harry drove me home. He remained as he had been all evening, silent.

'What was all that about?' I asked him.

He grunted. Then as we got to the Bush he said: 'Sorry. I didn't realize he was going to do that. Should've guessed. Sorry.'

'Well, it's not your fault. But it was quite hard work.'

'Sorry.'

'Harry – does he know that I was a belly dancer?'

'I don't know. Why? I haven't told him, anyway.'

'Don't tell him.'

'All right. Why not?'

'Some men get funny about it. You remember.'

He remembered.

I kissed him on the cheek and ran upstairs to my real life.

NINE

Lunch with Harry

The next morning was bright and warm and the world looked cleaner than it had for days. Three paracetamol and a pint of water last night had kept my head reasonably clear. Lily woke me in mid-conversation with herself about peacocks. I threw back the duvet with something not a million miles from elation, ambled into the kitchen to put her egg on to boil, and called Ben Cooper at home.

'Fifty per cent success,' I said. 'Come and get it. Now. Then I never want to see you again. Ever. All right?' I felt almost fond of him. It was over.

Then Harry rang, and said was I free for lunch? He sounded like himself again. He'd been like a different man with Bates the night before. Two-man Harry. One the one I'd known and loved; the other a reliable little crooked errand boy with no mind of his own. Yuck.

I thought no but I said yes. Lunch just for lunch. No invisible strings.

*

Cooper arrived as I got back from taking Lily to school. He was looking chipper, like one of those pink people who live in Spain and call themselves Brits. He peered into the cupboard that passes for my study as he came down the hall, fish-eyeing the print of Jean-Léon Gérôme's *Dance of the Almeh* on the wall.

'Tasty,' he said. 'Reminds me of you.' If I'd thought that he could make out the dancer's nipples (which are indeed visible if you look closely) I would have kicked him. It is irritating in later life how many men have seen you half naked.

I gave him the address book and didn't offer him coffee, though it was there on the stove. He sat down anyway, and admired the fading peonies on the kitchen table. I could see him taking in Lily's pictures on the walls: egg people and rainbows, with her name written in the corner in big round nursery school teacher's handwriting. The bottle of vodka was still there on the side from the night it all began, and beside it a cheque for three hundred quid that had arrived that morning from an ad agency I'd done some harem-style styling for.

'Nice place,' he said.

I may have been in a good mood but I wasn't getting into that.

'Here's the book,' I said.

'Nice life,' he said, looking round. I don't know why I felt vaguely threatened. No one ever appreciates how hard everybody has to work to keep their own little dream-home fantasies going. I didn't like Cooper being here in the middle of mine. I shouldn't have told him to come here. He was like a little lump of pollution in the middle of my carefully clean and airy world. My *enderun*. He seemed to seep nastiness.

'Only one I have,' I said. 'Mustn't grumble. But I've got a lot to catch up with, so you won't mind if I just . . .' I started to wipe the table right where he was sitting.

'Where's the diary?' he said.

'Locked in a drawer in the study,' I said.

'Should've got both.'

'I tried.'

'Didn't succeed, though, did you? And getting the one, now you'll have made him suspicious. And any luck with the computer?'

'I didn't even see one. I was there for dinner, you know, not as his secretary.'

'Silly,' he said.

He looked at me. I looked at him.

'Get a professional next time, then,' I said. Dammit. I'd thought it was over.

He sighed.

'And any news?' he said.

'He's leaving the country tomorrow night.'

'Is he? *Is* he?'

'And coming back in a few days.'

'Where's he going?'

'No idea.'

'Find out,' he said.

I said nothing.

He said nothing.

We were getting quite good at it by the time he made a big show of creaking to his feet.

'I'll have to think about this,' he said. 'I'll be in touch.'

I'll be out, I thought. I should have been out all along. I should not have got in. From here, a drink-drive conviction starts to look like a little thing, a thing no judge would hold against an otherwise decent woman. But now it's too late.

Ben left. Good riddance, I thought. If only it had been.

*

I met Harry in the Winfield because I didn't want anybody else in my flat polluting it. The Winfield is a club. There are no windows, just the heavy door with a little video camera so Liam knows whether or not to buzz you in. People go there to play snooker. I used to go there to drink late, in the days when I drank late.

Now I go there because Liam says, 'Hello there, Angeline' when I go in, and if you're working at home alone a lot that's nice. I go in the morning when it's empty and smells of old fags and cleaning fluid, and sit at the bar on a high stool to drink coffee and read the paper and exchange pleasantries. Liam will cash me a cheque if I need it. Sometimes I eat a toasted sandwich. Sometimes I peer through the darkened glass which makes up the far wall of the small bar-room into the great chamber beyond, where each huge table has its own low pool of light, and the green baize gleams, and the figures move in the dark shadows round the edge of the pool, puppeteers offstage to their long performing cues. It's a beautiful room. Nicotine plaster-work, heavy curtains, dark walls, dim corners. There are little telephones by each table and you can ring Liam behind the bar and ask for another vodka and tonic please. It used to be a dancehall years and years ago. Nobody knows how high the ceiling is because you can't see it. Brigid says she's seen it, when she leaves the fire-doors open first thing in the morning to clear out the faggy alcoholic smell of the place, but no one else ever has.

Liam, who wears polo shirts and has an ulcer, was none too impressed when he clocked Harry on the video entry-phone.

'He with you?' he said. I nodded, and Liam said nothing more, but I got a distinct chill. I knocked back my vodka and met Harry standing up already.

'Bye, Liam,' I said. Harry and he nodded to each other. I wondered why, and what I didn't know.

We spun up towards Notting Hill Gate in the Pontiac. He turned in and started trying to park in a street designed more for sedan chairs than for Detroit's finest.

The restaurant was built like a fishtank, full of laughing crowing rich and beautiful people. A pancake-faced public-school boy greeted Harry by name and took us to a desirable table. The ritual began to unfold: flicking non-existent crumbs from pristine white linen, ordering Chardonnay, sea bass, *lentilles de Puy*, glasses as clean as water, water sparkling or still, Madam?, napkins flick flick, fag packets on the table, matchbook contorted backwards like a fossilized sea anemone in the ashtray. It was late for lunch and most people were finishing their exquisite mousses and tiny coffees. Pancake-face sat down with us to take our order, took it, then came back and sat down again. He looked as if he had had a hard shift and was delighted to settle down for a breather, a glass of our wine and a nice chat.

'How've you been then, Harry?' he said.

Excuse me? That might very well be my line. He ignored me. Harry told him he'd been fine, thank you, and they talked for a moment or two about football. I considered leaving, but instead just murmured, 'I exist, I exist' quietly under my breath. Pancake-face was wondering where Harry went to school. The food arrived, brought by a lesser minion. Pancake-face finally left us to it, saying, 'Well, I'll see you later.' Harry registered my annoyance, but said nothing. I began to hate him again.

'I'm very sorry about last night,' he said.

'So you said,' I said.

'I don't . . . um . . .'

Well, if Harry's in difficulties when it comes to communication it's bound to be something delicate, emotional, or sexual.

'What don't you?' I said unforgivingly. He might as well imagine that this is all about whether or not I mind Eddie Bates fancying me.

'I don't think . . . I know from your point of view it's not any business of mine, and past history, but I don't think it would be a good idea for you to see Eddie again.'

Ha ha! I know why and you know why but you don't know I know! I've no intention of ever seeing him again but you don't know that either. You know nothing!

I played the innocent. 'Oh, really? Why not?'

I nearly added, 'I thought he was *charming*!' but decided just to land him with the bare question. Put him on the spot. Hypocritical sod. Protecting me, indeed. Anyway he knew I didn't find Eddie charming. He knew it automatically last night. We had been a thousand miles nearer to each other when he drove me home last night than we were now.

'Because he's not a very nice man.'

'How fascinating!' I cried. 'Do tell.'

He lit up a cigarette, despite not having touched his stuffed pan-fried squid with coriander and ginger. They looked much nicer than my onion and parmesan tart with radicchio and olive salad.

'I could tell you,' he said, smoke curling up his face, 'but then I'd have to kill you.'

Isn't it funny what can make your heart melt? That line had been a running joke of ours for years. We had worn it thinner than an antique coin. It always made me laugh. Always, always. And did now. I hadn't heard it or used it for . . . oh, all these ancient things.

I laughed. He laughed. He put his cigarette out. I took a mouthful of my food – it was good, actually. He smiled kindly at me. I said, 'So tell me.'

'Oh, it's nothing, he's just a pig with women. He has a wife who he's horrible to, and he's always here and there and running around, and I just wouldn't want to see him running around on you, that's all.'

Well, he was lying again, of course, but it was quite a sweet lie. Also I suddenly saw that he was jealous.

'You're jealous,' I said.

He put his mouth into a funny sideways shape, and pondered for a moment.

'Don't know,' he said shortly, as if the words were stuck.

'But you might be.'

'Don't know,' he said. And then: 'No right to be.'

I didn't want to talk about Eddie's real badness, whatever it might be, and I didn't want to talk about Harry's feelings, let alone how I felt about them. I didn't like all this having to choose between two dangerous lines of conversation.

So I said: 'Would you like to try a bit of this tart?' At least that's what I meant to say. What came out was: 'You bastard, you bastard, Harry, why did you do it you broke my heart and you ruined my fucking life and you never ever ever told me why, you bastard.'

He was as surprised as me.

I was as surprised as him.

We stared at each other for a moment.

'Sorry,' I said brightly. 'Not sure where that came from.'

'You know why,' he said.

'I don't know why,' I said.

'If you still haven't worked it out – it's not possible that you don't know why, so stop fucking around,' he said. He stared at me and then shut his eyes for a second. Then he almost shouted: 'Shit, why did you have to remind me that you disgust me?'

Disgust him? I disgust him? I disgust *him*? Disgust? What the fuck is going on with this boy? Hard words, Harry – hard words from a man who loved you, whose opinions you respected and liked and agreed with. Harry –

'Why?' I yelled. 'Why? What are you talking about? You keep not telling me things and I am not fucking around.' Suddenly it was just him and me, no context, no circumstances, no Cooper or Bates or anything. 'You just lie to me and blank me, you won't tell me why we're here and you wouldn't tell me why you left and you lied to Janie and you wouldn't talk to Mum and you are a lying deceiving fucking toe-rag' – toe-rag! I couldn't manage any better – 'and actually, last time but two that I saw you you all but called me whore and here you're pretending to try to protect me from someone you say is mean to women and you have no fucking clue – I can't believe you have a clue what you did to me I . . .'

I left the restaurant. I loved you so much, I loved you, I loved you. I was very confused. My brain was whirling and I was kicking a tree. A bus conductor looked at me. I turned west and ran down the road. Pigeons scattered before me. Harry wasn't following me. After a couple of hundred yards I sat down on a bench. My leg ached.

It is not possible to be rational when you are being emotional. The blood goes to different parts of the brain. Mutually exclusive.

Where did all that come from?

Oh, it's obvious. Oh, God. Blown it.

He must have known it all anyway. He knew I loved him then, we were just in love. Normal.

What is it I don't know?

He says, cool and rational, that it is impossible for me not to know why he left me.

That doesn't sound like a love reason. It would be quite possible for me not to know any complex emotional stuff going on in his head or heart. He knows for sure that he is unclear in that area. He's got that far, at least.

It sounded more definite. A thing, that I don't know. And didn't know then. A thing from then.

Who knows what happened then? Who knows what was what, then?

Not me. Harry, but he's not telling. Janie. But she's not telling.

Anybody *could* know. Small world like ours. Maybe everybody knows, and that's why it's impossible for me not to know.

Not to know what?

*

I spent the rest of the afternoon in the bath. I steamed my brain into oblivion and my body into a scarlet blob. I washed my hair and gave myself a facepack. I was about to sugar my legs when I started crying again and realized that I was thinking about the old days, when you'd sugar your legs because your lover was due. I emerged from a doze to find myself thinking about Harry's long flat belly in shadow under sheets. I dripped water all over the flat, wandering naked. I stopped to look at myself, scarlet, wet, older, with mascara sliding down my cheeks and wet hair plastering me. Kutchuk Hanem was only twenty-two when she was a flower not too far blown, and here I am, thirty-three. I used to be a fit woman, now I can't even run away. My scars were livid. Why do I disgust you? What do you mean, remind you? What have you been trying to forget? The same thing that I don't know?

Why do I mind?

I wondered for a moment if I still loved him. Well, I had to consider it. It was a possibility.

I decided no.

He was going to have been something else by now. Wasn't going to be a criminal, masquerading in the motor trade, toadying to villains. He was going to have been something good. Something intelligent. He was going to have been something better.

He isn't who he was when I loved him, and he isn't who he would have had to have become for me to love him still.

I just want to know what it was.

I dragged on my clothes and my good sense and went out to fetch Lily. We made flapjacks and coloured in and played woodland creature dominoes, and then Fergus rang.

'Sorry I couldn't get back to you,' he said. 'Now listen. Bates has never been convicted of anything, but he has been . . . associated . . . with every kind of improper import-export, including drugs, arms, pornography, illegal hormones for beef cattle, used NHS beds to China, chemical purifiers to Latin America, you name it. There is a wife who lives in Monaco, where he never goes, otherwise his private life, if he has one, is private. He moves around a lot, likes to play the grand gentleman but quietly. Lives in that other world, you know, where people are so rich that no one dare ask, because the purest it gets is a car factory founded on Nazi slave labour. Don't have anything to do with him. And don't feed me stupid lines about friends.'

'Why would a policeman want someone who was not a policeman to steal something from him?'

'Steal what?'

'Information.'

'Because he's fucking mad.'

'Any more helpful reason?'

'Because he can't get it legally, because he wants it kept secret. Angeline, what's going on?'

'I don't know . . .'

'Any policeman in particular?'

'Ummm . . .'

'Any policeman you trust more than me? Angeline, please . . .'

'A known to be, shall we say, flexible policeman.'

He was quiet for a moment.

'There is an amount of internal . . . sweeping and dusting going on at the moment. It's being done quietly. A number of officers of various ranks will be feeling nervous, and may wish to cover their backs. I think you should tell me what all this is about.'

'Well, I think it's over, anyway. I think, I hope. I'll let you know. And thanks.' I hung up, put Lily in the bath, got in with her, and we poured bottles of water over our heads until we were soaked. Then I chased her round the room with the hair dryer, covered her in anti-eczema cream, got into bed with her, and fell asleep.

TEN

Looking after Lily

The next day Lily wanted to wear her little pink gauze wings and tinsel halo to school. No problem. Brigid rang, wanting to borrow the car. No problem. Could she drop Lily at school, I wondered. No problem, she said. I like these days, when there is no problem.

And could she pick her up too, as I had to go round to Zeinab's? Of course she could, and she'd give her some tea with Caitlin and the boys. People who say single mothers are lazy scroungers should see Brigid on the go. She does the work of ten women, and half mine too, and no she's never had a penny off the state. She won't even take child benefit, that every married mother in an Espace takes as her rightful pin money. 'Helps pay for the piano lessons,' I heard one bray across Holland Park one afternoon.

I was measuring up the cloth to take to Zeinab when the phone went. I didn't answer. It was Harry, talking to the machine. He wanted me to call. I think not. Not yet. Maybe not ever.

Then Neil rang. I remembered enough to apologize to him for that row, shrunken in the perspective of time to a pinhead in my view, but perhaps still large in his. He said, oh, for God's sake, no, I'm sorry too. I didn't tell him anything about the results, direct or indirect, of his running out on me. I just asked him what Jim's legal status was.

'Why?' he asked.

'Why do you think?'

'Ah . . . well, a natural parent can claim a child at any time,' he said, 'and has a prima facie right to custody of the child. However, an unmarried father does not automatically have parental responsibility for the child; he obtains it either by the mother's written consent or by application to the court. That said, in any dispute the child can be made a ward of court by anyone, anyone at all, who is concerned for its welfare, in which case it will be a family division case and the judge will decide on the evidence of social workers and other witnesses what is in the best interests of the child, which are at all times paramount. You should remember all this, Angeline, we've been through it before. So what's happened?'

'Jim and his wife came to tea,' I said.

'Oh, yes,' he said. 'And?'

'And he wants her. They want her. They're applying for . . . oh, you know . . .'

'It would help if you could be specific,' he said.

Yes, and it would help if you weren't so bloody patronizing . . . cool it.

'They want her to live with them,' I said. I'm not so snappy. Really. Really I like it when he talks like a textbook, it's reassuring, and it's not so much for him to expect me to respond in pidgin textbook myself. 'Residence order,' I said.

'How much do you remember about how it works?' he asked.

'Just what we did before. Parental responsibility, residence order, all very straightforward,' I said.

'It won't be this time,' he replied. 'Look, we'd better meet. Have you told your parents?'

'Not yet.'

'Best get them along – they're a good weapon. I'll look out all the papers from before and do a bit of homework. Tomorrow, day after do for you? Um . . . in the meantime, think about things. They will have to prove Lily will be better off with them than with you, that's all really. Child's welfare is paramount.'

'But of course Lily's better off with me . . .' I began.

'Then there's no problem, is there?' he said, with that tone of patronizing irony that made me realize I was talking garbage – or at least that what was obvious truth to me still had to be proved in court, which was quite a different thing.

*

Zeinab and I got quite a lot done. Our client was His Excellency General Dr somebody or other whose son was to marry a princessling in Jeddah, and wanted five outfits each, matching, for three dancers. Why were they getting it done in London? For kudos. Because it would cost more. And for discretion's sake. I suspected the dancers were just for a private stag party. Many things are banned in Saudi, and many of them are available if you know where to look, so I'm told. Me, I wouldn't know, I've never been there. Why would I go to a country where a woman cannot go anywhere without a document signed by her husband or father – or son, or *grandson* if there are no other menfolk left – giving her permission? Even in Egypt, when I was there in the late eighties, when women who had been 'emancipated' for years were beginning to take to the veil again . . . that was enough for me. The Politeness Police coming round to check that all the dancers have their licences, and that nobody is too rude, and Saudi sheikhs paying off ageing performers to take the veil again on television. If a woman wants to wear *hijab*, fine. But when teenage girls are shot dead at bus-stops because their hair shows . . . that was Algeria. And all because 1,300 years ago Muhammad, who was employed by his first wife Khadija for over twenty years – she was his *boss* (and strangely enough Allah seems not to have revealed any of these woman-controlling truths until after she was dead) – said that people should only speak to *his* wives, his later wives, through a curtain. Women cause chaos among men. The idea that men might learn to control their own chaotic leanings, rather than control women, does not figure. But don't get me started.

About the worst of it is that Islam, a beautiful religion,

gets so warped, and so misrepresented, and . . . but don't get me started. This is not a simple area. Enough.

We'd worked out the colour schemes for the costumes, and the basic designs – they're always much the same, actually, for cabaret. There's the sweep of skirt with a central slit and a modesty panel down the front behind it (for one of my first costumes I'd forgotten to put one in, and my knickers showed, and I was sent home. It was a truly humiliating occasion, like a dream of going to school with no clothes on, when you're five). Then there's the veil, the headband and the bra. We were doing one with pantaloons and a little striped brocade low-cut waistcoat as well: old-fashioned, but very sexy the way the waistcoat lifts the tits under the muslin shirt. But generally they want to see leg.

I used to enjoy embroidering the bras: tiny detailed work, stitching and stitching like a Dickensian heroine ruining her eyes by candlelight, or the slaves making the robe for Oscar Wilde's young king. Then when your back feels like a fifteen-year-old rubber band, ready to split if you wriggle your shoulders, you look up and realize you have created an item of tiny glistening Faberge perfection, each sequin glinting, each bead just so, the whole encrusted with minute exquisite cheap tat, arranged to seduce and beguile with flash and glamour. It's a complete and gorgeous illusion. From a bag of haberdashery to the Arabian Nights, because I say so. Now I get someone else to do it. Zeinab knows a group of Sudanese women in Wembley who are incredibly neat and quick, and when they're not embroidering they'll sugar your legs, give you a massage, henna your feet, plait your hair – anything that quick little hands can do.

Some girls are so bosomy I have to charge them extra for the extra time it takes to ornament their bras. Some want such garish colours that I charge them danger money. I was embroidering one myself today, in sea-green and gold. Zeinab calls it harem when we sit and work together: one possible root of the word originally meant outlaw, lawless, meaning not so much bad as not covered by the laws of the world – a place with its own law. A place where you didn't have to fuss about what was meant to be going on outside. I like that.

In this atmosphere, the work should have been soothing, pleasant, but the outside wouldn't leave me alone, and the work just gave me time to brood. I didn't want Cooper to want anything more from me. I didn't know what I wanted Harry to want. I wanted Jim to disintegrate into thin air. And I wanted to know that which I did not know.

To take my mind off it I encouraged Zeinab to gossip and chat; unfortunately her subject for the day was how I had to have a child so that Lily would have company. Zeinab has an English husband and three beautiful sons, and tells me about once a day that she does not see why I of all people should take so literally what the prophet's daughter Fatima said: that the best of women is she who does not see men, and who they do not see. Today, for once, rather than denying it, I felt that Fatima was right.

I got back from Zeinab's at about five, expecting to find

Brigid and everyone having tea. No one was home. My guess was that they'd stayed at Brigid's – I couldn't remember what exactly we'd arranged – so I nipped down the balcony and down to the next floor to her flat. No one there. I nipped down two more floors and round to the other side of the building to Maireadh's. No one there. Of course, Maireadh would be at work. I ran over to the next block to see Reuben, Maireadh's boyfriend. He hadn't seen Brigid since yesterday. I ran down to the Winfield.

'She's not been in today,' said Liam behind the bar. 'Reuben was in last night though.' He gave me a vodka and tonic and let me use the phone. I rang home, rang Brigid's, rang the school (no answer), rang Maireadh's, rang Reuben.

Liam sent the other barman down to the post office to see if anyone had been in for a packet of sweets. Shirin at the post office said no, she hadn't seen any of them today. I suddenly thought Jim, then unthought it. He wouldn't. Possession may be nine-tenths of the law but a man making applications to the court wouldn't kidnap the child.

Stupid. I was panicking. Brigid would guard Lily with her life. She would never let anything happen to her. It's just a little domestic crisis. Something came up. Why didn't she leave a message? Ring in? I ran home to check if there was any sign that they'd been back – a coat, a half-drunk cup of apple juice. A note even. I couldn't remember how I'd left the kitchen that morning. There was my coffee cup, there was the cheque, the peonies still drooping. I put them in the bin. How can you lose a woman and five children? The answering machine was flashing three messages.

'Angie, I think we're going to have to do better. Give me a ring.' Cooper.

My mother, wittering a bit. Something about some stuff and she wanted to know what I wanted to do with it.

'Angel, it's Harry. Um . . . don't know where you are. Please give me a ring. Shit. Need to talk to you. I'll leave the mobile on. Please call as soon as you get this message.'

I rang Brigid, Maireadh, Reuben, Liam. Only Liam answered. Did I want him to speak to his pet copper, he wanted to know. No. I went out to see if my car was anywhere visible. No. I came back in and the answering machine was flashing again.

'Evangeline. Eddie Bates here. Guess what! Your little girl has popped round to see me. Why don't you come on over? Bring the book with you.'

I sat down for two seconds, just long enough to think that this was not something I could bear to think about, and I rang him.

'Marvellous!' he crowed. 'How lovely to be able to see you again so soon. Come straight on round.' The man is mad.

I didn't shout. I hardly did anything. I gathered myself up enough to say: 'Why do you have Lily?'

'She just turned up to see her Uncle Eddie! Isn't that nice!'

Why is he talking nonsense? Is it real nonsense or trick nonsense?

'I don't believe you.'

'Talking about peacocks! Lovely girl. Image of her aunt.'

She doesn't look like me. I have ordinary grey eyes and hers are huge and speckly. My hair is straight and fair, hers is curly and darker. Peacocks.

I thought he was leaving the country.

'I'm coming over.'

*

I rang Cooper. He wasn't there. I left a message with a secretary that I was going to Bates's house. I tried to make it sound significant and dangerous. It wasn't difficult.

I rang Harry. The vodaphone number I had dialled was unavailable, please try again later.

I rang the showroom. Jean said she'd give Harry the message.

I rang Liam. He said Brigid had rung saying she couldn't make it to work that evening. He said she had said Caitlin had had an asthma attack. She was at the hospital. She'd brought Lily home first and had left her there with Harry.

My mind went blank.

'With Harry?'

'That's what she said.'

'But she doesn't know Harry.'

'She said he was at your flat and Lily was pleased to see him so she left her with him.'

'What was Harry doing in my flat?'

'Search me,' said Liam.

'Why didn't she call me?'

'You weren't there,' said Liam. 'She thought Harry was all right.'

'Oh, Jesus,' I said. Harry had kidnapped Lily for Eddie Bates. 'I've got to go.'

Where to, Liam wanted to know, and did I want him to come with me? I said no but gave him the address and said if I didn't call in an hour would he get his copper to come there.

'You're a lovely girl, Angeline,' he said. Thanks, I said.

*

Brigid still had my car so I took a cab. The engine ticktick-tickticked as I got out on Pelham Crescent.

Eddie's house looked quiet from outside. Inside it was even quieter. He answered the door himself.

'Where is she?'

'Come in, come in,' he purred.

'Where is she?'

'Not in fact here.'

'Where is she!'

'I've no idea.'

He's no idea, I've no idea. Three years old. He could have put her in the attic and be lying through his smooth and pearly white teeth. Does he know I know that Harry had her? (Harry! What are you doing?)

'How did you know she was missing?'

He smiled.

'How did you know about the peacocks?'

'Have a drink, my dear. I'm afraid I've given Siao Yen the evening off.'

He was so smooth and so cruel.

'Really,' he continued. 'She's not here. I just wanted to make sure you would come, and having been disabused of the belief that you respond nicely to correct approaches, I had to use subterfuge.'

I looked at him.

'Really,' he said.

I believed that she wasn't there. You can smell a child's presence in a house. An extra light dimension, breathing, a warmth, something. I had lived with it, known it, taken pleasure inhaling it every night, had tried and failed and thought better of trying to describe it to people who thought I would resent not being able to go to nightclubs any longer. She wasn't there.

'Then where is she?' I murmured.

Bates was pouring himself a drink. 'Sherry? Champagne? What would you like?'

'To know where she is.'

'We'll deal with that all in good time,' he said. 'Now, I believe you have something of mine.'

'No I don't. I gave it to Ben Cooper.'

'Ah!' he shouted, almost gleefully. 'Ben Cooper! Of course, the missing link. I should've guessed. No reason for *you* to want to have anything to do with me, is there? *Is there!*'

I wondered how much he had had to drink.

'Darling girl,' he said. 'Darling girl. Really, how terrible that a wonderful girl like you should have to run errands for a little squit like Ben Cooper. Now how can I possibly make it up to you. You poor thing. Have a drink.'

He danced back to the drinks cabinet and pulled a bottle of champagne out of an ice-bucket. It was still dripping ice-mist. He'd got it ready. Taken it out of the fridge. For this occasion.

'I must go,' I said.

'No no no you mustn't,' he said.

'I have to find Lily,' I said, and moved towards the door.

'Stop or I shall shoot you!' he cried. Oh, Jesus. The gun. I looked round.

He was aiming the bottle of champagne at me, a white napkin over his arm, easing off the wire and tickling the cork. Thinks he's bought me, does he?

'Here we go . . . o-o-o!' He shouted. *'Wheeee!'* and raised the bottle. The cork flew out and hit the Chagall in the middle of her merbelly.

'You're not going anywhere, though, are you?' he whispered to me. Oh, god, he's mad. I took a glass of champagne and drained it.

'You don't have my child and I don't have your book,' I said, gently. I was suddenly glad of the practice I had had over the past weeks in not panicking. Jim didn't panic me; this won't panic me. Jesus, I've been not panicked from Casablanca to Istanbul, and via the back roads too. I shall deal with it. That's what women do. Deal with it.

'I don't give a hoot for the book, my darling, not a hoot.

Poor little Ben, trying to prop himself up with irrelevant objects.' He was laughing. I wasn't.

'What have you got me here for, then?'

'To tell you off. Or maybe fuck you. Or maybe both.'

Change the subject, change the subject.

'You kidnapped Lily to tell me off?'

'Didn't kidnap anybody. Took advantage of circumstances, that's all. But if you don't behave I'll have her killed. Now. Put this on. Let's get in the mood.'

'I'm leaving now,' I said.

'I know where she is!' he said. 'You don't know that I don't! You just behave, and then little Lily will be back in Mummy's arms.'

'Where is she, then?'

He just tutted, and handed me a bundle. A bright, shimmering, flouncy bundle, pink and silver. It was a belly-dancing costume. It was one of mine. I shook it out: the chiffon skirt, the silver embroidery, the long veil with its silver edging, The bra fell heavily to the floor. Pink and silver, encrusted with rhinestones, stained with sweat. I remembered it. I had made it. I had given it to Janie.

Janie. She had loved my dancing, wanted to join in but she was no good at it. She'd had a few classes, got excited about it and then given up, as she so often did. Janie, what is going on? Janie, my sister my friend my sister I miss you I miss you I miss you. Not that you would have been a blind bit of good in this situation. Idiotic Janie.

'Put it on!' he urged, smiling. 'You can change in the hall.

I'd like to maintain the mystique. It's quite safe, no one will see you, there's no one else here.'

'Where is Lily?' I said. I was getting boring.

'Do as you're told,' he said.

I went into the hall. I sat on the pristine carpet at the bottom of Vivien Leigh's staircase and pulled off my boots and my jeans. Only half an hour before Liam calls his policeman, I thought. Harry may have Lily but he won't hurt her. He may not be the man I knew but he won't have become someone who hurts children. Will he? No. No . . . No. Liam said Brigid said she liked him. Pleased to see him. God, Brigid, you weren't to know.

I'll dance for him; if he tries it on I'll kill him. Like Morgiana, Ali Baba's servant girl, when she recognized the captain of the forty thieves having dinner in their house, disguised as a venerable merchant with a long white beard. After cooking and serving the dinner, she decked herself in all her finery, anklets and bracelets with silver bells, her long amber necklace and her golden girdle with the jade-hilted dagger hanging from it in its decorated sheath, all the little presents Ali Baba had given her before for being so clever and killing all the thieves when they were hidden in the oil pots. She had antimony round her eyes, which glittered with a feverish light, and henna on her slender hands and feet, and her shining hair fell down to her gold-circled waist. First she danced like a happy bird, the dance of the handkerchief, and the Persian dance, and then she started the slow, swaying, dance of the dagger, with Abdullah the black slave playing the tabor, strange and mysterious, and she pulled the blade from its silver sheath, waving and gesticulating as she plunged it first into imaginary enemies and then, as the rhythm quickened to a feverish pace, whirling and whirling and enchanting the eyes of the men, she plunged it into the old merchant's heart.

Her prize was Ali Baba's son Ahmad. I'll get ten years. Self-defence. I'll never see Lily. Mum and Dad will look after her. It'll be all right. I'll just be a crippling failure at the only thing I ever wanted to do, that's all. Not the end of the world. Lily doesn't need me. One hair of her head, one tear on her face. I promised her. Promised Janie, promised Lily.

The carpet tickled my arse. I stood to pull on the skirt. The fact that the waistband still fitted gave me momentary and irrelevant pleasure. I took off my top and fastened on the bra. There was a simple ring in my belly where the ruby ought to be. (Little Egypt came out struttin' wearing nothin' but a button and a bow, oh oh oh oh; she had a ruby in her tummy and a diamond big as Texas on her toe, oh oh oh oh . . .) I must have looked like crap, untanned, unsugared, unshaven, unfit, red lines round my waist from the jeans, with my scars and my very slightly withered left leg which nobody but I noticed. There had been no muscle there when it came out of plaster. Nothing. Bone, skin, and a sort of amorphous floppiness. A shocking horror to a dancer.

Why am I worrying about the details of my appearance when Eddie Bates has kidnapped my child? Because it prevents me thinking about what is going on. What *is* going on? Find out. Find out what he wants. He's mad. Let's hope it's something simple.

If he just wants sex will I?

Why should he get what he wants?

Would I?

For Lily?

For even the chance of helping her?

Where is she?

And if I do, what will he do?

And if I don't?

I don't do that.

I am not a prostitute for any price.

I don't do it for money, I do it for love.

For love of Lily?

I don't trust him anyway.

I don't do that. I don't sell sex.

I can dance, though. I can dance for anyone.

Standing in the hallway, I heard the music start up inside. A very familiar sound. My music. A tape of Ahmed's band. 'Our little percussionist,' he used to call me, because I controlled my anklet bells so beautifully – I could dance with them silent for fifteen minutes then with one flick have them shiver and ring; I could carry the stillness which is the heart of the dance. Everything I know about controlling my little cymbals I learnt from the Sufi dancers at Al-Ghoury. I loved the idea of being a musician *and* a dancer. Dancing the music.

Why does Bates have a tape of Ahmed's music? He has planned this. What has he planned? Is this just a complex and ineffably maladroit pass? He didn't know I existed before last week. Why does he have Janie's costume? Does he know who I am?

I am not going to be tormented. I am not going to run away and be stalked around this big house by a man who wants my body. In the film of my life Sharon Stone is not going to be me, whimpering, while Robert de Niro points a gun to my head and cries: 'Dance, bitch, dance!' I will not teeter on frightened high heels for anyone's gratification.

I decided to assume the worst. He is psychotic, he is obsessed with belly dancing, he's going to try to rape me because I am a belly dancer. Jesus, he's mad. He might want to kill me.

How does he know I'm a belly dancer?

Did Harry tell him? After I asked him not to? Why am I still fantasizing about trusting Harry?

The music grew suddenly louder as the door opened.

'I'm waiting!' came his playful tones. He sounded just like Lily on the loo: 'I'm ready!' Wait for the end of the introduction, fool. I was still trying to work out if the gun was good news or bad news. He didn't know I knew it was there. Only half an hour.

The *takasim* started, and I walked in. He might be ready but I was not going to dance until I was. The audience does not control the performance. The dancer has all the strength, the mystery, the power. When I dance I am not me; I am every dancer who was ever lusted after by a man who could not have her. I am protected. I am other.

I was waiting for the *nay.* Still, calm, in control, my very stillness speaking full-on disdain. Ishtar, Scheherazade, Salome and Morgiana, I thought. *Awalim* and *ghawazee.* My feet became the rhythm, my hips became the rhythm, my spine began to rise out of it, the lifting, rising, elongating. The stillness in motion. It was all still there. Here we go.

*

Scheherazade had her sister to help her, you know. Every morning it was her sister, Dunyazad, her only permitted visitor, who asked leave for a story to be told to beguile the cool hours before the daylight reddened the sky. She set Scheherazade up, morning after morning, for three years, neglecting her life and her youth to bring her sister through, to hand her up each time again on to the trembling tightrope of that day's chance of survival. Every day, with that psychopathic caliph, Shahriyar, wife murderer, serial killer, the two women sat and talked their way out of it, one because she had no choice, and one because she loved her sister. Picture them in the courtyard, surrounded by luxury, fountains, jasmine, soothing sherbets, slaves, silks, enchanting the madman. Entertaining as though their lives depended upon it. And when Scheherazade danced, she ravished wits and hearts and ensorcelled all eyes.

Of course by that stage Dunyazad was the last remaining beautiful maiden in the city, all the others having fled in terror. If Scheherazade failed, the Sultan would take

Dunyazad as his bride, and she too would be slaughtered the following morning.

And of course it was all a woman's fault in the first place: if Shahriyar's first wife hadn't been having it away with a handsome black eunuch he would never have had to kill all the others, would he?

*

Bates was an easy audience. I gave him a top-class show all the same. I was dancing for me, and gave him the works, as far as I was physically capable of it. The tape was about twenty minutes: pacing myself, and bearing in mind my leg, I might be able to do an encore, and then Liam would be getting help over here. I could not think of any way to detain Bates other than dancing for him. Anyway, didn't he have a flight to catch? I would dance, and something or someone would turn up, and then we would knock Bates out and tie him up and have the police take him away and find Lily and Harry and everything would be all right and I'd only have Jim to worry about, and how in God's name all this started.

I love to dance. The falling inside. I can enjoy it even like this. Bates enjoys it too. He's practically slavering. This is a sexual thing, I was right. Can't take his eyes off me.

I turned on my heel and flicked my hip at him as I drained my champagne glass. Flick flick flick, figure eight, and on. My muscles liked it. My leg felt OK. My soul was rising and my spine became so long that I gave him some back arching with teasing hands and draping hair. He lit a cigarette.

Set fire to me would you? Bastard.

His cigarette is nestling in his crotch. Oh, you dirty old bastard. Why don't you just get it out and have done with it?

I don't like to be humiliated.

I moved back to the drinks cabinet and poured pepper vodka into a shot glass, shimmying the while. She's OK, nobody's going to hurt her. When I turned round to him he was lying back on the sofa, visibly touching himself up, and I had the glass between my teeth for the rose-water trick. I danced for a few more minutes, closing my eyes. If he gets his dick out he's getting pepper vodka all over it. That probably hurts, doesn't it? Otherwise, his face.

What good would that do?

Make me happy.

I opened my eyes.

He got his dick out.

'Oh, you *bitch!*' he shouted, but he didn't seem unhappy about it. 'Lick it off.'

Oh, dear, he thinks it's a game. A lovely little sex game.

I don't want to play sex games. Yes, well we all know what you don't want. It's not exactly the point at the moment.

Yes it is, it's exactly the point.

'You dance a million times better than your sister but I wonder if you're as good as her at *that*,' he said, leaping to his feet, sneering, laughing.

Don't stop dancing.

I *can* think and dance at the same time. OK, just take

it in. Keep moving. I backed off from him. Retreat and regroup. Sway figure eight, sway figure eight, sway figure eight. Simple, repetitive movements. My leg is my pivot, my axis, I am rooted, moving, but rooted. He cannot unbalance me unless I let him. Think. Slowly.

He has seen Janie dance. He has had sex with Janie. I don't know which surprises me more. Keep dancing. Don't let it show. God bless you, body, keeping on.

I can't think this through. Accept the facts. Accept that this is more complex than you thought. Dance.

He came towards me, dick in hand. If this were a movie I could just kick him in the face, try to overpower him. Would it help?

He's not angry. He's bigger than me.

I just want to know everything. He won't tell me anyway.

He might.

Can't talk and dance at the same time.

If I stop dancing, can I avoid sex? Can I turn it to talk? He likes talking.

I whisked away from him, back round to the drinks cabinet (black, oriental, inlaid with mother of pearl, little figures of fishermen under droopy dripping trees; very pretty).

'More champagne?' I said, smiling nicely at him. The music continued and I found myself still moving in time with it. I was trying to keep the mood, the enchantment, the sense of audience and performer. I shouldn't have broken it with my spitting trick. Regain it. An audience knows its place. Put him in his.

'Oh, yes,' he said.

He was astonishingly easy to please.

'Sit down, I'll bring it to you,' I said, and he did. I sashayed across, jingling my coins, swinging my weighted cloth.

'Here,' I said, so dutifully, so charmingly, and knelt in a semi-formal dance attitude not quite at his feet. I didn't catch his eye. He thought that the energy going on was sex; he thought that at any moment our mutual attraction was going to burst into flames and I was going to fall into his arms. He didn't recognize that the spirit coming off me was pure defensive aggression. He thought it was . . . a lust power game. He thought I was withholding permission because withholding permission makes it so thrilling when you give up. His arrogance was my strength.

'You lovely girl,' he said, and took a draught from his glass. 'You sweet ambiguous creature.' I smiled dreamily. Sherbets and courtyards and fountains and jasmine. If I'm to be his whore I'll be an *Almeh*. I am intelligent and learned. We'll talk. This is my game too.

'Tell me about Janie,' I said, as if it were all quite normal.

'Lovely fuck,' he said. 'Does that make you jealous? I can imagine that might be the sort of thing to annoy a girl. Specially a girl like you. Proud sort of girl. I do like that. Janie wasn't very proud, was she?'

When I was young I used to read Barbara Cartland novels on the bus and there was always a scene where a middle-aged nobleman with a fleshy mouth and corrupt eyes would proposition the red-haired heroine in the library, enchanted by the flashing of her angry green eyes and the whiteness of her throat. Any moment now he was going to call me a plucky filly and express his intention to tame me. This is all very old stuff. I don't need to lose my temper or my bottle over this. Here I am and this is what's happening. No, Janie wasn't proud. Irritable, but not proud.

'I didn't know you knew each other,' I murmured. I don't need to react. We're here because of Janie. If I set him off, he'll talk. (They only want to talk, half the time.)

'Oh, I know everyone,' he said. 'And so did Janie!' This he found very amusing. I didn't see why and couldn't seem to bring myself to smile along.

Suddenly he leant forward. 'I know you,' he said. 'Don't I?'

I said nothing.

'Do you know me too?'

'Yes,' I said. He was talking about the fire. Or about some deep inner link we had that neither of us could deny and that would any moment bring us to our destiny – bed. Git.

He was talking about the fire.

'You should have taken the money. The fact that you didn't made you far more interesting to me. Even a whoring man like myself has a deeper yearning for a girl who won't take money. You can't rape a whore, you know, because you know she'd sell it anyway. Raping a whore is just stealing. No fun at all. Making an honest girl take your money is much more fun. But making an honest girl give it to you . . . making her want it . . .'

How much can I smile at this crap? I can smile. I smile.

'You do, don't you? You're so polite and you know it and you think I can't tell. Poor little Harry! What could a simpleton like him have done with you! What a waste! Well, you won't be wasted any more, my dear, don't worry.'

He was dimmer than I had thought. If he thought Harry a simpleton then he was very dim. Or perhaps he believed only what he wanted to believe, which even the cleverest can do. No, I should not imagine him to be dim.

'But you didn't take my money. So I knew I would have to take you. And here you are! After all those poor imitations . . . poor Janie. Not that she wasn't a lot of fun. Lots of fun. And it wasn't just the money for her, you know – I can tell. She liked it too.'

I'd been avoiding it but it was coming through too clear.

He was looking at me – at my face, not my body.

'I believe that perhaps you don't know about this.'

I said nothing.

'Did you not know?'

Is this what I didn't know?

'Oh! Oh, God, oh, I'm sorry,' he said.

He *was* sorry. He slipped to the floor beside me and slipped his arm around me and held me. 'I am so sorry. I am so sorry. I wouldn't have told you like this. I had no idea you didn't know. No idea. I am so sorry, here, here.'

I was crying. He was giving me a handkerchief. He was being kind. It was honest – it was the first honest reaction I had ever seen in him. That was how I could tell.

I was thinking about his reaction to my reaction to what he had said. I was not thinking about my reaction. I was not thinking about what he had said. What had he said?

He had said that my sister was a prostitute. He was telling the truth.

The doorbell rang.

'Get dressed, darling, get dressed. Go on, go on upstairs. I'll be with you in a moment.'

He was being absolutely kind. I scurried, grabbing my clothes from the bottom of the stairs. In the bathroom I swiftly changed back into my jeans, washed my face, and considered stealing his gun. I decided against. I don't want to kill anybody.

I know my power in my dance clothes: the power of sex, of legend, of mystification in rhythm, of performer over audience, the hypnotic female power over men's desire. The power of that unreal woman that I become when I perform, that painted, costumed archetype, that dream woman we all can be. But, Lord, I preferred the freedom of jeans and boots. I was more and more convinced of Fatima's argument. Both the seer and the seen are cursed. Put a man and a woman together alone and there is always a third person present: the devil.

Downstairs, I heard voices. Harry's voice. Behind him another, a man's.

I emerged calm. Eddie was saying, 'No, I don't think so,' to a uniformed policeman. Harry was standing back, separate.

'Well, sir,' the policeman was saying. He seemed to want to come into the house. I swept down.

'Miss?' he said.

'Hello?' I said.

'DC Tom Stevens, miss. Is there any problem? We had a report . . .'

'Oh! I don't think so. No!' I acted bemused, and gave Bates a big brave thank you, darling, now-we-have-bonded smile. I think he thinks I'm his girlfriend now.

'You're sure now, miss?' said the copper.

'Everything's fine!' I said. 'Why, did someone . . . ?'

'I'm so sorry to have disturbed you, sir, miss,' he said. 'Seems to have been a time-waster. If anything does turn up, you give me a ring . . .'

He got my drift, and left.

'Bloody snoop,' said Eddie.

'Harry,' I said, 'where is my daughter?'

'At Brigid's, with Maireadh,' he said, 'having her bath.'

'You don't know where Brigid lives,' I said.

'Lily does,' he said. 'Where the fuck were you?'

I asked Eddie if I could make a telephone call. Of course! I rang Brigid. Lily said Brigid made her eat her fish fingers even though she had only wanted bread and jam. I said quite right too. Brigid came on the line and said she was awful sorry about the mess up and was Lily to spend the night only she had to go back to the hospital to Caitlin but Maireadh would be here with the boys. I said I'd be over shortly and if Brigid had left I'd sort it out with Maireadh and was Caitlin OK? Brigid said yes it was all just a bit sudden but they'd had her on a nebulizer and she was sleeping now and they'd be letting her out in the morning almost certainly. I said thanks, Brigid, for everything, I'll speak to you in the morning then, and Brigid said she liked the look of that Harry, by the way. I looked at Harry. He was looking blank.

'I must go, Eddie,' I said.

'Of course, darling,' he said, and gave me a fond kiss and a proprietorial hug and a reassuring squeeze, and said, 'I'll call you later,' just to put a cherry on it. 'As soon as I get to Paris.' Paris! 'Don't be too upset. We'll talk it all through. Just get some sleep.' It was as if he had suddenly slipped into a different part. His kindness at my shock may have been true, but this was . . . another stroke in the repertoire. Changing channels on the radio. The same actor saying lines from a different film. There's a fault somewhere.

'I'll drop you,' said Harry.

Eddie looked up.

'I'm going back to Ealing anyway,' Harry offered.

'What did you come for anyway?' said Eddie.

'Oh – to drop this off.' He gave Eddie a packet. 'Thought you'd like it as soon as possible, and I was coming this way.' It wasn't quite too much explanation, but I knew it wasn't the whole story.

I started for the front door, thinking that I'd just hail a taxi. Harry was immediately with me.

ELEVEN

Learning

It must have been eight o'clock. The evening was beautiful: sunlight on London, the white stucco, the blue sky, the gentle warmth. I was almost surprised to be alive. I was tired. The vodka and champagne were beginning to retreat, leaving their refugee trail of dirty mental detritus behind them: a cloudiness, a taste in the mouth, an underbelly of fear. The laurel leaves of the gardens gleamed beneath their dust. A couple walked by, party clothes, laughing. Lilac. This weather was unbelievably lovely. My legs began to quiver a little. I was going to be stiff tomorrow. This sunlight. My mind and heart suddenly filled with an image of a window, a bed, a shaft of late-afternoon sunlight. It made me catch my breath.

We walked on.

'Here,' said Harry, and handed me into the Pontiac. He drove me home without a word. I dozed a little. I don't know to this day if his silence was anger or concern or

. . . if I had been thinking, I might have thought that he had just lost interest. But I wasn't thinking, and he wasn't talking.

He dropped me outside the flats, and just said good night as he pulled off.

Maireadh said Lily was sleeping, so why didn't I leave her? I looked in on her, head to toe with Michael in his bed, peaceful.

I ambled home. I could hardly walk. The weather made me want to cry. The lilac made me want to cry. My legs made me want to cry. Lily made me want to cry. Harry made me want to cry. Janie.

Once Janie and Robbie Turner had tied me up in Mrs Harris's garage and left me there when it was time for tea, and Mum had said, 'Where's Evangeline?' and Robbie had giggled but Janie had said, 'We tied her up in the garage and left her there so she'd be late and you'd be cross with her.'

We used to go out on the old fire escape outside Mum and Dad's bedroom window and twine the pale green tendrils of wistaria round and round the rusty iron railings, and sing, 'Oh, soldier, soldier, won't you marry me with your musket, fife and drum?' Each spring last summer's tendrils had turned to dry twigs, except for a few which had turned to strong living wood, twined tighter than we could ever undo. The living tendrils were velvety, silver, tender. We would discuss our wardrobes for when we were queen of the world. Janie wanted a wedding dress made of magnolia petals. I wanted a tunic and hose made of wistaria velvet, and a helmet carved from flint. Our beds would be emerald green moss cushions. Or hammocks, from willow leaves. Once she threatened to burn my teddy at the stake. We found a dead frog and tried to give it a Viking funeral on the duck pond in Holland Park but it wouldn't catch fire.

The last time Janie lied to me was . . .

. . . was when she stole something from me, what was it? Sweets . . . a lollipop or something. A sherbet dab! She ate half of it and put it back and said she hadn't, and then that night she crept into my bed in tears and said she had, and she was so sorry.

Janie was always greedy but she didn't lie.

When could she have been a prostitute without me knowing? How?

And how was I so certain it was true? I was certain. Knew it. I knew she had it in her.

She always had boyfriends, or at least boys to get off with if she wanted, when I didn't – not that that proves anything. She never, as we termed it, went all the way, not until Colin, but she'd be in the parents' bedroom at other people's parties, snogging, or pretending she was going to but not actually letting him, while I'd be sitting in the sitting room with the other three unpairable-off social cripples: the fat boy, the spotty girl, the little brother who wasn't really meant to be there, and me. Janie was off tormenting a big brother, a boy from sixth-form college, someone with a bumfluff moustache and platform boots and a greatcoat from Lawrence Corner. Someone who smoked and drank Newcastle Brown. Someone with an earring. I'd be waiting till 11.30 when the hosts' parents would come back and we could go.

'What a great party,' Janie would say, her eyes huge under their gleaming eyeshadow and her lip-gloss (flavoured) smudged. I'd tell her to tuck her shirt in. I couldn't not go to parties because it upset Mum.

Was it when I went away? I knew everything about her before that. She didn't quite know everything about me. But I knew everything.

She liked rich people. Liked comfort. But she wasn't luxurious. Couldn't afford to be. The banker disappeared and Jim appeared. Then Harry and I broke up. Then I went away. Then I came back and she and Jim weren't getting on. She wasn't a runaround, but she had admirers. The dinner dates and the married men who emerged from the woodwork when she started work (PR! I ask you! She went to work in PR!). Lots of men she would have nothing to do with. How we laughed about them! She'd ring me almost every night when she got in, to mock them. We were cruel, actually. Young, good-looking and cruel.

Perhaps after I went away. I wouldn't have known what she was doing then. Couldn't have known.

She wasn't wildly rich. She wasn't on the street. Was she lying to me all along?

What about after I got back? There were three-odd years, before she was pregnant. But we were friends, sisters. Her moaning about Jim, me with my pathetic attempts at a lovelife without Harry. Her with her job that I laughed at, me dancing and biking, turning up at her office on the Harley to have lunch with her, and her pretending that she didn't notice that her colleagues were impressed . . . Her and me on the phone at all hours, analysing what had become of our university friends – she always knew, I didn't because I was running round with my 'Swarfega friends', as she called them, my post-Harry dim-but-beautiful biker boyfriends. 'When did you last sleep with a man who didn't have a motorbike?' she'd ask. 'No, don't try to remember, I'll tell you. It was George, 1983. That nice Greek boy.'

How could I not have known then? Or did she stop it then? When did she stop? Did she stop?

How could she do it? Why did she need to?

She never lied before. I was the liar. I'd lie quietly and gently to make things seem right. Rewrite history, subtly to my own advantage. Deny things. That infuriated Janie; when she would say that the parents had ruined our lives by sending us out of our own class, by experimenting on us, and I would say what's the problem? Everything's fine!

What have I rewritten about her?

She wasn't on drugs. That I would have known. But then you'd think I would have known she was selling herself. You'd have thought.

It's a very curious sick feeling to realize that you know nothing.

I made myself a cup of tea and pulled a chair out on to

the balcony in front of the front door. The petunias gleamed at me in the dusk. A few late big children called to each other from the courtyard below. Someone somewhere was cooking a fragrant meal: ginger and garlic and hot oil. I could hear cutlery clinking through an open window; voices from a television, the bong bong bong of the nine o'clock news. Still quite light. The last western sun catching me. I wanted to go and get Lily, just to hold on to her. Better for her, though, not to be my comforter tonight.

And if I didn't know, who knew?

Oh. Harry knew.

And thinks I knew too.

*

The telephone went. I answered it before thinking that I didn't want to talk to anybody. It was Mum. I took the phone out on to the balcony, dropping my cigarette because Mum doesn't know I smoke.

Did I get her message, she wanted to know. Oh, yes, sorry.

So what did I want to do?

About what?

About the things.

What things?

The things she'd said about.

Sorry, Mum, what things are they?

Things of Janie's, in the box, in the attic. Honestly, girl, where's your brain?

Things of Janie's.

Now of course I immediately read this as a communication from beyond the grave. Sitting here asking the wide blue yonder what the hell was going on three years and more ago, and suddenly there is a box, with things in.

'I'll come and get them. What's in there?'

'I don't know, love. I haven't looked.'

'Do you want to go through them together?'

'For me personally I'd like to throw them away. But I knew you wouldn't think that way so it's here if you want it.'

'If I find anything do you want to know?'

'Find what?' she said.

'I don't know . . . anything.'

'There's nothing . . . but I knew you'd want to look.'

'I'll come on out then.'

'What, now?'

'Yes – why not?'

'Where's Lily?'

'She's staying the night with a friend.'

'At three? For God's sake, girl . . .'

'It's OK, Mum, she's just around the corner and she's fast asleep. I'll be round there before she's awake in the morning. It's OK.'

It was OK.

*

Enfield. What a godawful place. They had a nice little place, though, a leftover vicarage from the days when it was a village and not just a section of the A10. It was easy getting up there at that time of night.

Dad opened the door, and gave me a glass of wine and a big hug. Loves me so much now he's lost the other half of me. Loves me for bringing up Lily, because otherwise he and Mum would have to and he likes his quiet life. Loves me for being brave and strong and never asking him for money, which he always offers even though I know that they don't have much now.

Dad was a journalist. Sports. When we were kids he scurried around the world reporting, interviewing, Rome, Brazil, World Cup, George Best, Carnaby Street. Mum just taught all day, but Dad had shaggy hair and a leather jacket, and stories. Dad in his thirties in the sixties. He bought into a bar and a football company with a retiring footballer. Did all right. Groovy Dad, neat resigned sensible Mum. Not without humour.

Now he watches cricket all day and night because they've got satellite. Mum wishes they hadn't. She sits up in bed reading modern feminist literature until he comes up. Her bedside table has Angela Carter, Maya Angelou, Jeanette Winterson. She says it's nothing to be surprised about, she taught English and read *The Well of Loneliness* when she was fifteen, and knows all about Rebecca West and H. G. Wells. She says that emotions are all very interesting. She doesn't like them in reality though. She likes life quiet. Like Dad. They do the garden. Twine their wistaria.

There is a big picture of me and Janie on the sideboard,

looking young and excited, dressed up to go to a May Ball. They did have our graduation photos but Janie took them down saying we looked horrible and hysterical, which we did. So there we are in 1984 make-up and 1984 party clothes, clutching each other in that same early evening early summer sunshine. She'd come over to Cambridge for May Week, then I'd go over to Oxford for Eights Week. Darling parents disguising their pride in their own ways. Dad taking the piss because his dad worked the market at Spitalfields ('Lucky none of us'll be going to heaven because I tell you your granddad wouldn't know what he'd helped to produce here'). Dad made the money, but he was never quite happy with what he'd paid for, for us. Mum acting like it was the least you could expect, if you educate girls right and take them on camping holidays to France in the Ford Anglia to broaden their minds, and bring them up right with all the opportunities and work hard to pay for them they'll do right by you too, and there's no reason why they shouldn't. Because Mum, of course, didn't know the half of what we got up to. And she will not know about this.

Mum was in her dressing gown. 'You didn't have to come all this way now,' she said.

'I wanted to.' It wasn't ten yet. Dad looked settled in but he turned down the sound on some fuzzy sporting fixture from a long way away.

'Have you eaten anything?'

I laughed. Mum looking after me. Sooner you than

anyone. Normally I laugh at it, tonight I just think how nice, how kind, how lucky I am that I love you and you love me.

'I'll have a look in the fridge.'

'There's some chicken on the stove.' She always has too much food in the house. Lettuces going slimy, hotpots unfinished, because she still can't quite take it in that the two hungry girls don't turn up with all their hungry friends any more.

I foraged a plate of chicken and potato salad and went off to find the box. It was on the landing upstairs: just a dusty old tea-chest, standing there looking as out of place as the Tardis.

'Are you going to open it here?' It was Mum's voice behind me, discouraging.

'I'll take it home.'

I ate my salad and got half-involved with the match on television. This is a model self-improved middle-class home, and there is a dark secret even behind the tragedy over which we have triumphed. Mum picked up her book: Isabel Allende. I may have come all this way but her duty was done now: inquire, feed, that's it. No need to converse. That's all right.

Only it wasn't.

'Mum,' I said.

'Hmm?'

'I've heard from Jim.'

Dad picked up the remote without looking at me and

switched the television off. Mum put her book down and stared at it.

'And?' said Dad.

'He wants her.'

The silence hung, palpable, unavoidable.

'Bang go the savings, then,' said Dad.

I felt I should apologize. 'Sorry,' I said.

'No one's shooting the messenger,' said Mum. 'When can we see Neil?'

'Tomorrow?'

'Whenever,' said Dad.

'Tomorrow afternoon, then. His office. I'll give a ring with the time.'

Dad grunted. Mum had closed her eyes. I kissed them each on the cheek, and I left.

When I got home there was a message from Eddie, full of sweet nothings.

TWELVE

Flowers from Eddie

I woke at seven and could hardly move. After the previous afternoon's unexpected dancing my abdomen felt like half-set cement and my legs had seized up. I sprayed the length of them with Ralgex and popped an arnica tablet, then pulled on some loose clothes and went round to Brigid's. Lily was still asleep, tucked in among the fair heads of Brigid's boys in Brigid's big bed. Aisling was just getting up in the sitting room. Brigid emerged from the boys' room, where she had been sleeping on one of the bunks. 'They all came in with me,' she said. 'So I had to go in there. Musical beds, I ask you.'

I climbed in beside Lily and the boys and fell asleep again for about two seconds. Lily woke me, telling me I smelt funny. It's the Ralgex for my legs, I told her. Why do my legs want Ralgex, she wants to know. Because they're stiff, I explained. 'Stiff as a three-legged dog,' she said, and then she wanted to be a puppy, and I had to be the mummy puppy, and then everyone woke up and we all ate rice krispies.

I took them all home and crawled into a hot bath while they started to build a pirate ship in the kitchen. My legs were loosening up a bit. I longed to get back into bed but I tried to do some work instead. Concentration nil. I called Neil and arranged to see him at two. It was Saturday but he'd go into his office specially for us. Indebted indebted indebted.

Once the subject was raised in my mind I couldn't let it go, so I started to write my affidavit, child voices ringing through from the kitchen.

'Lily Gower was born prematurely, as a result of a crash in which her mother died . . .

'Lily Gower has lived with me for three years and two months, since her mother's death and her birth . . .

'Lily Gower's mother, my sister Janie, was killed when . . .'

'Lily Gower has lived with me since she was born, when her mother died in a motorcycle crash. The police report of the crash is attached herewith. No blame was apportioned and no prosecution suggested or pursued . . .'

Why am I using words like herewith? The law speaks a different language, writes yet another one. I can't pretend to understand it just by flinging in a couple of those words that only ever appear on paper. Apportioned, suggested or pursued. Oh, Mrs Pompous.

'Lily Gower has lived with me since she was born, when her mother died in a motorcycle crash. The police report of the crash is attached. It was an accident and there was no prosecution.

'Lily was born by Caesarean section and her mother, my sister, died soon after. My parents and I took responsibility for Lily. Hearing nothing from James Guest we – her grandparents and I – felt that he had abandoned her. We heard nothing from him for the next three years, except when he asked to be registered as Lily's father on her birth certificate, which we agreed to do because we believe that a father, even an absent one, is an important figure in a child's life.'

No point in mentioning how Dad said he'd sooner shoot him, or how without even discussing it we gave her our surname, not his.

'She has met her father once, on x May this year when at his request he and his wife came to tea at our home. She was not told that he was her father, as not knowing Mr Guest's intentions I did not want to upset her.

'If Mr Guest wants to have contact with her, we will do everything in our power to help and make it a constructive thing for Lily. For Lily's sake we would make genuine efforts to forget the past and help her to build a good relationship with him.

'Lily has a full and happy life. She knows that her mother died, that I am her mother's sister, and she treats me in all respects as a mother. As she grows older and asks more questions I will do my utmost to be honest and kind with her regarding the fact and circumstances of her mother's death.

'Her relationship with her maternal grandparents is close and friendly. It helps her to place herself, and to see that her mother being dead does not mean she is without a close and loving family. We all visit each other regularly and take holidays together.'

Well, we do.

'They and I have shared parental responsibility for her since her birth, and there has never been any difference of opinion. Her vaccinations are up to date and her development is normal for her age. She suffers from eczema, and has treatment for it constantly in the form of special bath oils and creams, and attention paid to keeping the flat dust-free.

'She attends a local Montessori nursery school for twenty hours a week, which she enjoys very much. She has friends there and is attached to her teachers. When not at school she is cared for by me and occasionally by our close friend and neighbour Brigid O'Hara whose family of small children, particularly the daughter Caitlin, are devoted friends of Lily's. The children are constantly in and out of each other's homes. As Lily is an only child, I would be loath for her to lose these friendships.'

They are at this moment destroying my kitchen. I went through to sort out a dispute about the dustpan.

'As I work from home and am relatively well-paid, I am able to make a decent living and spend a lot of time with Lily. Her well-being is my only responsibility and commitment. I work only enough to keep us reasonably off. We cannot afford expensive habits, but we do not need them. Ours is a happy and secure home.

'Those who meet her see a normal and happy child. Since the trauma of her birth and the loss of her mother she has lived a very steady and secure life, with a gentle routine, constancy of relationships and no major disruptions. Going to a new home with different people would, I believe, be very damaging to her, both in the short and the long term. Losing the person she thinks of as her mother, having lost her blood mother, would cause her untold unhappiness. My own unhappiness at losing her would be as deep, but of secondary importance.'

Oh, God. Is this the sort of stuff they need? Is it too personal? I just want to give them facts, but it reads as if I am laying it on thick. All that hoovering and self-sacrifice. Well, is Jim going to do it? Is Nora going to stop high-flying to do it? Or are they intending to hire someone to love and care for her?

It is all facts. I'll ask Neil.

*

The doorbell rang. It was a small Birnam wood of madonna lilies, star-gazers, roses, tuberoses and greenery, wrapped in an acre of sparkly clean cellophane and crimson satin ribbons. It reeked of rich flowers and expense. The delivery man was invisible behind it.

'Miss Gower? Flowers,' he said, unnecessarily.

The card – about a foot square, heavy vellum – said:

'I hope my marvellous girl is feeling better. See you later. EB' The writing was not a florist's loopy biro with a circle over the i instead of a dot. It was squiggly, very black, very small. Each letter seemed to be having trouble deciding what direction it was meant to be taking. If I hadn't doubted his sanity anyway, I would have at the sight of his handwriting.

I took them in and suffered a quick ontological crisis. They were so gobsmackingly beautiful. I don't get sent flowers very often – like never in the past five years. But I hated him and hoped never to have to see him again.

I got the big plastic bucket and put them in it, on the kitchen table. I would leave them there while I decided whether or not to throw them out with contempt, and by the time I decided they would probably be dead. It's not their fault who sent them.

They sat there, smelling at me.

I rang the parents and told them what time to go to Neil's office, then stared at Janie's tea-chest for a while.

*

The meeting with Neil was constructive. He sat behind his enormous desk in his elegant offices in Canonbury and told us not to worry about his fee . . . but I know he costs two hundred pounds an hour, and whether or not the meter was running officially there would be some kind of debt run up somewhere. It made me uncomfortable but inclined to be efficient.

'The child's welfare is paramount,' he said. 'The court will decide what is best for her. Jim and his wife—'

'Wife?' said Mum. 'What wife?'

'He has a wife,' I said. 'Name of Nora. Cold-looking, clever, a career woman. Nice clothes, if you like that sort of thing.'

'Which you don't,' said Dad.

'It's a good move on his part to have a wife,' said Neil. 'A lone father would be unlikely to get a residence order. Anyway, they have to persuade the court that Lily would be happier and better off, in the long run, with them. Their main weapons will be that they are richer, that they are a married couple, and the fact that Jim is her blood father. They may also try to denigrate your capacity as a parent, Angeline. Our main weapon is that you have been bringing Lily up for three years, and have done a good job. On the whole courts like not to change a situation unless there is a clear and definite benefit to the child to be had in doing so.

'Courts are not that impressed by money alone, unless one side is actually incapable of providing for the child, and even then they may order the wealthier parent to maintain the child while it lives with the other. The fact that Jim has given you no financial help will tell in your favour. They are impressed by emotional stability. Jim has been married for two years – we could argue that that is not long enough to prove stability, and mention that marrying within a year of the death of a long-term girlfriend, the mother of one's child, does not bode well either . . . Ange, you will have to explain your emotional situation . . .'

'My what?'

'You heard. The court will want to know – and has every right to ask – whether you have a boyfriend or boyfriends, live-in or otherwise, what your sex-life is, how it affects Lily . . .'

'OK, OK.'

Mum was looking at me.

'What?' I said crossly.

'Do you have one, love?' she asked curiously.

'You're not the court,' I retorted.

'Ange,' murmured Dad.

'It'll be easy,' I said, shrugging like a bad comic. 'No. No, no and no.'

'They won't necessarily like that. They'll be thinking that you might get one at any time, and that could be disruptive. You'll fall in love with an oaf and forget all about Lily in your blind infatuation. Single women are always vulnerable, you know.'

Was he saying it just to annoy? Getting at me, because I wouldn't have him? Reminding me what a good qualification having a nice rich lawyer husband would be in this situation? I remembered him three and a bit years ago saying 'and get married'. He was looking at me with sweet frank eyes.

'I'm only saying what the court will think, Ange. Not what I think.'

Yeah.

'Well. You can just promise them that that won't happen. Look ugly and sexless on the day . . .

'And then we can point out Nora's dedication to her career, and question whether she would be happy to sacrifice it; we can doubt that Jim is about to become a house husband. Courts prefer one person to be caring for a child, and are not impressed by strings of careful arrangements with third parties, or by nannies, au pairs, nurseries etcetera. If one of them is suggesting giving up their job to care for Lily then we may be in trouble as you, Ange, will need to continue working. However, we can say that they have no way of knowing what they are letting themselves in for, and it probably won't work. We can also point out that Nora, who it would most likely be, is not Lily's blood parent, is in fact a total stranger to her, and connected only by a father she does not know, and who abandoned her. We can go big on the abandonment. They may say that Jim wanted to be settled before he claimed her, in which case we can say why wait two years then? Or he may claim that he was too upset after Janie's death, in which case we can laugh at his naivety and explain gently that caring for a child does not actually allow you to be so delicate – the child's welfare comes before our emotions. Our big advantage is that we can prove that your way does work, while they can do nothing but promise and project. We have three years on our side.'

'How nasty is it going to get?' said Dad suddenly.

'Depends how much they want her,' said Neil. 'At the moment we don't even know why they do. Jim has never struck me as the paternal type, but Nora is an unknown. It could be her, persuading him. If they lose, and choose to carry on applying, they can carry on applying, as long as they have new information to bring to bear, and as long as the courts let them.'

'So what happens next?' asked Mum.

'A court welfare officer goes and checks Angeline out, makes sure you've got loo paper in the bathroom and that kind of thing . . .'

'Oh, Jesus,' I moaned, softly.

'. . . then the court will want to see Lily, then we have the hearing. In the meantime we get our affidavits together.'

I gave him what I'd written up already, muttering excuses and qualifications. He called in an extraordinarily beautiful girl of about twelve, who seemed to be his secretary, and asked her to photocopy it three times.

'Everybody take home a copy and make a note of what they think should be in it,' he said. 'No need to be shy. Blow your own trumpets. People sometimes try to be polite or generous in these things, and there's really no point. No one else is going to be. Come out all guns blazing.'

We all stood up and made polite noises. Neil seemed terribly impressive and prosperous with his big desk and his knowledge, in command of his own world. I rather envied him it. It must be wonderfully comforting to know who you are, and what you are. I couldn't even define my profession in the affidavit. 'What do you do for a living,

Miss Gower?' is about the most difficult question anyone can ask me. If only I could say: 'I'm a lawyer.' Or: 'I'm a doctor.' Or: 'I'm a dustman.' Then everybody knows where they stand. How nice and cosy that makes them all feel. We understand each other. We are safe.

But I don't and I'm not.

God, am I envying security and a steady job? What are things coming to?

I handed my parents down the stairs and then told them I had to nip back and say something to Neil, I'd be with them in five minutes or did they want to go on. Mum flustered a little and Dad shook his head in an 'Oh, women' gesture, and they decided to head back to Enfield. I said I'd ring them later and bounded back up the stairs to Neil. Or tried to – I bounded two steps before my legs reminded me to try no such thing.

'Neil, one thing,' I said.

'Umm-hmm?' he said, hardly looking up from some papers on his desk.

'That night we had the argument . . .'

'Oh, Ange, that's all right, really, you don't need to . . .'

I hushed him.

'I had to get the car out of the traffic,' I said. 'Now I'm not telling you this to make you feel bad – I'm not.' I wasn't. 'I was well over the limit and I got pulled.'

'How the hell did you manage that?' he said.

'I turned the wrong way down Rupert Street. And I got pulled.'

'That's not going to look good,' he said. 'Bugger. At all.'

'Yes, well . . . It's worse. Or not.'

'What?' he said.

'I wasn't prosecuted.'

'And you're not going to be?'

'Umm . . . no . . .'

'Well, that's all right then,' he said.

'Not exactly,' I said.

'Why not?'

I felt like a five-year-old in front of the headmaster. I am not five. Neil is not my headmaster.

'I arranged not to be prosecuted,' I said.

'Um, Ange?'

'I had a word with . . .'

'Shut up,' he said.

'What?'

'I . . . You are not being prosecuted. That's great. I'm really glad, and thank you for being so frank. Your lawyer should always know everything that you think is pertinent to the case. It's great you told me that. Now, the welfare officer will call you to arrange a time to come round, she'll probably want to see Lily's school, and your parents, and maybe your friend, whatsername, so you'll need to help her arrange all that. Be nice to her. They have lots of power. I'll speak to you later. Bye, now!'

He swept me out as if I were a strange cat eyeing up his goldfish. It took me no time to realize that any notion I had of confiding all in Neil was a complete no-no, and about three seconds to realize why: if he knows, and someone asks, he has to tell. He was protecting us both. I could tell him, but then I'd have to kill him. Oh, God, Harry.

Strolling down Canonbury Square towards the tube I suddenly felt the burden so heavily that I caught my breath. I so wanted to tell somebody – anybody – all that was going on. Just talk it through. There were so many strands, so many clouds of half-formed stuff that either was relevant or wasn't. And relevant to what? If I talked it through, I could perhaps work out what the questions were and then try to find out some answers. Were there even any questions?

How do we beat Jim?

Why was Janie a whore?

How do I get Eddie off my back?

Ditto Ben Cooper?

What is it with Harry?

Yes, there were some questions.

It was unreasonably and unseasonably hot. As I reached the station the combined smells of plane tree, hot pavement, lilac and tube air became too much for me. Even in Canonbury the air is bad, even with all these leafy squares and tall Georgian windows. I went into a reverie of tall Georgian windows and wide clear pale wooden floor; a grand piano, shafts of sunlight, a bowl of roses, real fat droopy roses from a garden, falling apart in scented abandon like an ageing mistress, like Kutchuk Hanem, not etiolated stiff-necked one-bloom-a-stem Dutch greenhouse and chemical roses. Lily drawing under the piano, me playing Chopin. I can't play the piano. Get a grip.

*

I went straight to Brigid's to get Lily, and then home via the swings and the ice-cream van. It was jangling out Lilliburlero. Lily wanted the version with the old lady who went up in a basket, seventy times as high as the moon. She made me sing it in the street.

*

When we got home Ben Cooper was sitting on the doorstep.

'What's up?' I said, not going up to the door.

'Need a word,' he said, looking for the first time I have ever seen tired, drawn and uncomfortable. Well, my doorstep is not comfortable.

'Well, not now, Ben, I've got to get Lily her tea and then I'll be putting her to bed . . .'

'It's important,' he said.

'So's all that,' I replied, chirpily but firmly.

The look he gave me was almost beseeching.

I ran through the options quickly. I'd have to talk to him.

'Come back later,' I said. I didn't want him in the house, invading my *enderun*; I couldn't ask Brigid yet again to sit for Lily.

'Lily will be asleep by eight or so. Come at eight-thirty.'

'I don't believe this,' he said, lumbering to his feet. 'I

don't believe I'm being pissed about for a child's bedtime.'

'Did we have an appointment?' I said frostily, and sashayed past him, bringing Lily with me. I hate it when people assume that children don't matter. I hate it. 'And please mind your language.'

That made him laugh, at least. Bitterly, mind you.

Lily and I went in. She said, 'No one was pissing near him, Mum'; I said, 'Pasta or . . . er . . . pasta?' realizing that I hadn't been to the shop in days; and Ben dragged himself off down the balcony like a dying elephant. I'd been afraid he was just going to park himself on the step till I was ready.

*

I made him sit on the deckchair outside the front door.

'What do you want?' I said.

'Stop being rude to me,' he said. 'We must talk. Can't we go somewhere?'

I wasn't letting him back in my flat. Not in the evening. Not alone. Not him. Not anyone. How much it was a question of aesthetics and domestic purity I don't know. True, I'd felt him polluting my dream home earlier, but now I just felt very very wary. Enough changeable men had been frightening me. And I really didn't fancy hearing his comments on Eddie's bouquet.

Out of naughtiness, I suggested the Winfield. Ben was not keen on the Winfield, and I knew why. In the evenings it was often full of off-duty police, talking out of turn and mouthing off. Once I'd heard a fat-arsed drunkard saying that he was going to get that Linford Christie . . . they were the kind of police who couldn't bear a successful black man. Ben would be right at home with them in many ways, but he would be reluctant to speak his mind with them as earwigs. I counted on that. I wanted him to drift away, fade away, not exist any more. As I wanted Jim to, and Bates. Stupid way to behave, actually. People don't do that when they still want something from you. And Jim wants Lily, and Bates wants my body, and Ben wants something else which is perhaps about to emerge. Oh, well, let it.

'No,' he said. 'I don't want to go there.'

Why was I bothering to be nasty to him in these little ways? I knew we weren't going anywhere. It just amazed me, yet again, how he had forgotten Lily's very existence, and the fact that you don't just go out and leave a kid on its own. People just do not think beyond themselves. Me, of course, included. I don't think much past me and Lily.

'Stay here, then,' I said, making the invitation as uninviting as possible. 'Drink?'

I got him a glass of whisky. He was looking truly terrible. I told him so.

'Yeah, well, you would too,' he said. He looked at his whisky, as if it were something he had seen before somewhere, but couldn't quite place.

'It's whisky,' I said kindly. 'You asked for it.'

He grunted.

'You drink it,' I explained.

Suddenly he shifted in the low, undignified deckchair. With the perkiness blown out of him I could see how out of shape he was. It was as if his confidence had been the only thing keeping him upright. He kept on gazing.

'Ben, this is all very nice but it's late and . . .'

He cut me off.

'When I asked you to help me out before,' he said, pulling himself up as best he could out of his slump, 'it was on the off-chance. It wasn't a very good idea, and it wasn't very likely that you would be able to achieve anything for me. I shouldn't have done it but I did . . .'

'Why, as a matter of fact?'

'Shut up,' he said. 'What?' He thought for a minute and then said, 'Because you were there.' That's what he said last time. Then, with a half-smile: 'And because I like to have women dancing around doing what I tell them.' Then his thoughts overwhelmed him again.

'All right,' he said, 'tell me everything you know.'

'I know bugger all, Ben! I have not a bloody clue what's going on.'

He gave me an old-fashioned look.

'I know that Eddie Bates is some kind of crook and Harry Makins is his minion, running some car business for him, but I can't imagine you don't know that. I've gathered that Eddie is also some kind of a perv – well, he fancies me – and that something of some kind is presumably going on involving you, or that you are interested in, but you certainly know more about what it is than I do. I know he likes to eat nice food and have a line of coke with his brandy after dinner and his maid is called Siao Yen. That's it. Oh and he went to Paris on Friday night. Or said he was going to.'

'Paris. Did you believe him?'

'Sod knows. I don't know and I don't care.'

'Who'd he go with?'

I just looked at him.

'Paris.' He went into a dream. 'And he's coming back?'

'As far as I know.'

'Do you know . . . no, well, perhaps you don't. Listen . . .'

More heavy pausing.

'Eddie likes you,' he said. A statement, not a question.

'In a way,' I said. 'Does he trust you?'

'I shouldn't imagine he knows the meaning of the word.'

'Oh, yes, he does. He just doesn't trust it. As you wouldn't, in his shoes.'

'Anyway I stole his address book. Of course he trusts me.'

'Does he . . . how was he when you went back there?'

'How do you know I went back there?'

'You left me a message, remember? Reporting in, like you're meant to?'

'He was . . . fine. Keen to be better acquainted.'

'Oh, good . . . Not angry about the address book?'

'He said he couldn't imagine why even a little squit like you should imagine he could shore himself up with something so unimportant.' I took the opportunity to embroider a little.

'And what did you make of that?'

'Nothing. None of my business.'

'Do you not feel it becoming your business?'

'No.' I made sure not to pause before saying it. I did not want Ben knowing how very much I felt it.

He sighed. 'We were always friends, weren't we, Ange?'

What? I hate you, Ben, surely you know that?

'I always felt for you over what happened with Janie. She and I were good friends, you know. She helped me out too, *you* know. And I helped her. Oh, yes. There were times when Janie and I really . . . I was always a friend to her.'

'I'm not Janie,' I mentioned.

'No, no, of course not. But you know, things are getting a bit . . . interesting . . . these days and I'd like to know that I can rely on someone . . .'

'Well, you can't,' I said. 'Not on me, anyway.'

'It's a shame you said that.'

He lumbered up out of the deckchair and turned to lean against the balcony wall, looking back at the chair in disgust. He swallowed his drink in one.

'OK,' he said. 'Here's the deal. You are to continue on good terms with Eddie. You are to see as much of him as possible, keep him liking you, and ring me twice a day or more to tell me how he is, what he is doing, where he is going, who he is seeing, what they are saying, what he is wearing, where they are eating and who is serving the drinks. I want the colour of their socks. I want all sightings of documents, particularly passports, address books, diaries, any kind of contact list. I want copies of anything you can get copies of – tapes, videos, business papers. If you have to fuck him, so be it. And – before you blow your mouth off – if you don't, I shall be releasing your arrest for drunk driving to the relevant authorities, along with details of how you tried to bribe me, and sending details of the whole thing, plus your relationship with Eddie Bates, to Jim Guest, his lawyers, the social worker on your case and the court, out of a spirit of public duty.'

'Why should Jim be interested?' I asked blandly. 'What are you talking about?' Useless of me, really.

He gave me his old patronizing chirpy look. 'And to let you know just how serious this is to me, I'm going to tell you just a little of what is going on.'

I could see it was hard for him. I wondered why he had decided to tell me. Then I realized. He wanted to frighten me.

'It is quite likely that Eddie will soon be leaving us. He may be going to rot his days away in a horrible little cell; he may be going to Casablanca or Buenos Aires. It is not yet apparent. If the former, he intends taking me with him. If the latter, the possibility of the former will always remain. I need a little insurance. There are things I know about Eddie which others do not know. A little proof – which you will get for me – will cover me. And as long as I am covered, so are you. If I go down, I intend taking you with me.'

'If he goes to prison anyway, it won't matter what you know.'

'The things I know, Ange, are rather different, and rather worse.'

'What are they?'

'Why should I tell you?'

'Because you're sending me off to spy on him? Because you're encouraging me to sleep with him?'

'Sleep with him enough and you'll probably find out for yourself,' he said. 'Oh, come on, Angie, just use your wiles. You don't have to know. Better you don't know. Just stick close, gain his trust if you can, let me know when he shows signs of going anywhere, and pinch anything significant.'

'How will I know what's significant?'

'Ring me and ask. Ring me anyway. And if you get into trouble ring me and I'll come and rescue you.'

'Yeah, like you did last time,' I muttered.

'What last time?'

'Yesterday!'

'What happened that you needed rescuing from yesterday?'

'Nothing,' I said. 'Nothing you need know about.' A pathetic kind of yah boo sucks. 'Anyway, he's not going to trust me an inch. He knows I nicked the address book for you.'

'Have you noticed he's a little mad? I don't think he will hold that against you. Not by your report.'

'I'm not going to do it, Ben.' Suddenly I saw the image of flame, and Eddie's face. 'It's a completely mad idea. It's not going to do you any good and it's putting me in an impossible position . . .'

'Kiss bye-bye to Lily then.'

'Please don't do that.'

'If you won't save me, why should I save you?'

'It won't save you from anything.'

'It might. Think of yourself as a straw, and me clutching at you.'

I wondered if I should tell Ben about when Eddie tried to set fire to me. To show him exactly why I was reluctant. To give him a chance to let me off the hook. Give him a chance to redeem himself, and me, and call a halt to this whole stupid thing. What the hell, give it a go.

'Ben . . . once when I was dancing, in a restaurant, um . . . a man tried to set fire to me.'

'And?' he said.

'It was Eddie.'

'There, you see!' he said. 'You do know something after all!'

And so do you, I thought. And knew all along. And don't give a shit. Yes, Ben, we were always friends.

'That's why I'm not doing it.'

There would have to be another way. We could emigrate. Take her to Egypt. Zeinab's mum would put us up for a bit. I could . . . I could . . . oh, shit.

'Call me tomorrow, love,' he said, and left.

'Well, you've only yourself to blame,' I said, and thanked myself for my kind and sympathetic words.

THIRTEEN

Janie's Tea-chest

I spent Sunday prowling. I prowled into the kitchen. Then out again. Into my study. Down to Lily's room. Into my bedroom. Out again. The phone kept ringing and I didn't answer it. I put on a tape of Umm Kalthoum, the most beautiful voice in Egypt and the most Egyptian of voices, in an attempt to soothe. When talking came on the answer-phone I put my fingers in my ears and sang loudly along with her.

'Why don't you answer the phone?' said Lily.

'Because I don't want to,' I replied.

'I'll get it, then,' she offers helpfully. She loves the phone, thinks it's for talking nonsense into. 'Hello, Banana-head,' she says.

I discourage her. And prowl back into the kitchen.

'Can we go to the park?'

Good idea. Go to the park before I go off my trolley. I cannot actually think of a single person with whom I am on pure and honest good terms. Everybody I know, either I'm lying to them, or they're lying to me, or I'm concealing things from them, or they're concealing things from me, or I hate them, or . . . God, the list is endless. For a moment I wished I were a Catholic so I could let it all out.

I prowled back into my study and stared at the most recent bank statement, lying unopened on my desk like a not-to-be-trodden-in cowpat. I have to do some work. All my Lily-free time is being taken up with this stuff. In three months' time there's going to be a sudden hiatus in cheques coming in. I've got nothing outstanding to do . . . I should be out chasing things up, putting myself about. Oh, shit, yes, I have got something – an unopened jiffy bag under some papers suddenly reminded me that it was a book I was meant to be reviewing. Two hundred pounds! When the hell is the deadline? I'll take it to the park, put Lily in the sandpit and start reading it. Birds and stones, birds and stones. Then I won't hear the telephone, and it'll take my mind off Cooper's ultimatum, and how incredibly angry I am with him.

*

That night when Lily was asleep I went into my study and decided it was time to brave Janie's tea-chest.

I'd already been through her things when Lily was tiny: pinching her history books, sorting her clothes for the charity shop, discarding her gubbins ruthlessly. Or trying to. I'd sat with my leg stretched out in its plaster, and Mum passed me things and Zeinab helped. I don't know if it was harder physically or emotionally.

Her things were so like my own yet so different. Her clothes were better than mine, yet equally badly kept: eighty quid Ghost dresses that looked like Indian rags from the Portobello because she'd never hung them up or had them cleaned; beautifully cut leather jeans going dry and musty because she didn't wear them any more. (At least I always kept my bike leathers in good condition.) Beautiful little Kenzo suits for work – I'd never realized that she had so many because they all looked exactly the same to me, grey and disgustingly tasteful. She'd been wearing them at twenty-three, and we all laughed at her for wearing grown-up clothes. They all went to Oxfam. In Ghana they call second-hand clothes *Obroni we tvu* – the white man died. Her make-up – again expensive, again in a big mess, leaky bottles of Clinique foundation, powder falling about, lipsticks bought in 1984.

Everything which might have been something I'd have had, I'd put in with my own things, and let them get jumbled up, and absorbed them into my life until I forgot what was originally whose. Thinking about those tribes where you take on the strength and qualities of the person you have killed. I didn't want her strengths and qualities. Let alone her weaknesses. But I didn't want to lose her. Anyway I didn't kill her in competition, in battle. I just happened to be there. Well.

I'm not going to start on that again now. Everybody in

the whole wide world except for me says I was not to blame. But what do I care what people think? I should have been able to prevent it. Enough. Enough.

Anything identifiable went. I gave Zeinab her beautiful long black velvet dress. Threw away all her food, her half-used box of tampax.

We'd cleared the flat in two days. I'd set aside some things for Lily: the sequin jacket, her diaries, her letters, a bit of jewellery, lots of old unwritten-on postcards, photographs. She wasn't sentimental like me and there wasn't that much. I poured drops of cedar oil in the bottom of a wooden chest, then sealed it all up, rather romantically.

Her underwear, come to think of it, had been quite something. I binned it all except a completely delicious black bustier-corset affair from Rigby and Peller, a good five hundred quid's worth I found out when I took it there to have it adjusted to fit me. Even the adjustment cost fifty quid. We were very nearly the same size, but my waist was a little smaller. The dancing did it. I'd forgotten all about that item. Haven't had much call for that sort of thing. I was glad now that I'd never got round to wearing it for any dirty passionate true-love tryst of my own.

I just wanted to know what she did and with whom. How it worked. Did she hang out on street corners? I think not. Expensive hotels? Company flats? Escort agencies? Hostess bars? Did she have a pimp? How the hell did she get into it?

Quite apart from why.

Who would know?

I went and rang Harry. Hung up after one ring. I was doing the box now. I'd put it off for days. I'd thought that we'd done it all, back then, but I was wrong. Go on, dig up bones, off you go.

I didn't know what was in this box, or why. Neither Mum nor I had packed it up. I supposed it must have been old old stuff that Janie herself had packed away years ago. I was expecting feather boas and old invitations to drinks parties at Magdalene, photobooth pictures of laughing young people with long hair and plucked eyebrows, all squashed in together. I couldn't have been more wrong.

I dragged it into the kitchen and pondered the best way in. From the top, girl, don't put it off. Just pull off that bit of blanket – God, I remember that, it was one we had as children, green tartan, we used to use it for a kilt when we played Bonnie Prince Charlie. OK, back and forth through the layers of time. Start pulling things out. It wasn't actually that full.

Under the blanket was a large old-fashioned black metal money box, the kind with a red stripe around the edge and a ring in the lid and little trays you could take out. I put it on the table and opened it. It was unlocked. It had no trays. Inside it was nothing but wads of fifty-pound notes. I blinked, and closed it again. Opened it again. Closed it again. I put a pile of newspapers on top of it. It still showed. I took it over to the old armchair in the corner and tucked it under the seat cushion, at the back, in the black hole of old upholstery. I put the newspapers on the seat. Then I put the kettle on.

This is how I lie, you see. If I put a cushion and a pile of newspapers on something then it doesn't exist and I don't have to deal with it.

'I just want everybody to be happy!' I'd say, and Janie would look at me and say, 'Well, they won't be, will they?'

I took my cup of tea back over to the chest. Another piece of our childhood blanket covered a stack of videotapes, each in a white card cover, and labelled only with a date, in Janie's large semi-italic handwriting. I pulled one out. The sticker too had nothing but a date, written with one of those nice fine black felt-tips: 21 March 1989. My twenty-sixth birthday. I'd been in Casablanca. I'd run out of money and was dancing in a hotel there, a tourist hotel. The northerners were rather disappointed in me; they hadn't wanted a blonde belly dancer. Local guys thought I was great, though, and I worked there for four months, I suppose, till the manager decided that he had had enough of my virtuous refusals, and that I should accept that I really was his own harem, and proceeded to try and enforce it. The owner of the hotel came to me in tears saying that all he wanted to do was sack the manager for his behaviour, but he couldn't because the manager's brother-in-law had put up half the money for the investment, and he was mortified but he could not protect me. I have seldom seen a man so sad and ashamed. Casablanca.

I shook off the memory and pulled the tapes out of the

chest. There were about ten. I hadn't ever known Janie to use a video camera. Perhaps they were just TV things. But no – her TV tapes had gone to Oxfam with her movies and her exercise tapes (including Belly Dancing for Fitness and Fun – we loved that one) three years ago. All the labels on those were scribbled and Tipp-Exed and scribbled over again. I stacked the tapes up and supposed I'd have to go over to Brigid's to have a look at them.

Apart from that there was a bundle of what looked like bank statements and a small jewel box. Inside the jewel box was a little stash that even I could tell were not rhinestones. It was flashy-looking stuff. An English lady would not wear this. Ivana Trump might. A couple of diamond rings, cut ugly and modern; emerald earrings that looked like something out of a cracker, but weren't, and three heavy gold chains. I'd never seen Janie in any of it, which was hardly surprising. I'd no idea what it was worth.

So. She'd been good at her job and well paid. So she'd put her pension in a chest and hidden it under the bed. My little sister the Ouled Nail. I drank my luke warm tea and looked out the window at the petunias. They were looking the worse for wear.

I don't disapprove of prostitutes. We all sell something, that's what you realize when you grow up. You sell your time, your strength, your skill, your knowledge, your looks, your youth, whatever you have. Harry's sold his soul. I sold my body for years. Who am I to say a woman shouldn't do that? Then I see, what . . . brutalized emotions, exploited teenagers, greedy cows who do it because they think it's easy, and they have no contact with their own hearts anyway. I see women who have no alternative: that's all they have to sell. I see women who assume it's all they have to sell because they have been told so often that they are worthless. I see men living off the back of it. I see violence and loss and heartbreak and lies. I see Noor.

The independent woman who does it and can do it, who has the strength, I say good for her. But I don't believe her.

And Janie? Janie wasn't that kind of woman. I very much minded her doing it. Because I believe – OK, I know – that it fucks up your emotional life and your relationships, it puts you in danger of disease and violence, it makes you disrespected, and it makes you lie. She lied to me and now she would never be able to explain, to apologize, and I would never be able to forgive. One lie like that makes a mockery of everything you thought was true. My sister, who may have been lying about everything else too. My sister, who was my confidante for thirty years. Did she laugh when I moaned on to her about the men at the restaurants who would make passes at me, and offer me money? What did she think when I told her how I scorned them, and hated them, and couldn't believe they would be stupid enough to imagine I would take their money? (I was very young then. And so was she.) And later when I was a little clearer-eyed, and told her that I knew now they didn't imagine anything about me except what I looked like with my knickers off, did she laugh at my carefully protected virtue? Or did she cry?

Here it was fucking up her relationship with me when she'd been dead three years.

Did Jim know what his girlfriend was up to?

If he didn't that's a reason for her keeping this secret box of goodies. And her career was another reason, of course, for her always refusing to live with him. She always said it was because of the violence. And was she lying about that? Did she make that up as an excuse to me, to explain why she didn't live with him? No. I saw the results. Yes, but I didn't see them being delivered, or who delivered them. Or why.

You see? One lie, and you set off a train of doubt and mistrust. Not because you were a whore, Janie, but because you never told me you were, I now don't know if I believe that Jim used to beat you up.

That's stupid, said Janie.

'No, it's not, it's completely rational,' I said.

'Rational's got nothing to do with it,' she replied. 'You know it's true. And if you don't you should do.'

'I know that you told me. But what's that worth now?'

'You have no faith, do you? No faith in me, no trust . . .'

'Well, how am I meant to? Now?'

'You never did anyway – you just wrote me off. You thought my job stank and my boyfriends were gits, you weren't even interested in me . . .'

'I bloody was!'

'If you had been you would have known what I was doing. How could you have not noticed that your own sister was a prostitute? Eh? You should have known!'

'What do you mean I should've known?'

'You're my sister, you're my friend. You should have known.'

'You should have told me.'

'I shouldn't have needed to. If you were a proper friend you would have known. I thought you did, half the time.'

'How could I?'

'A real friend would have. If you had been thinking about me and paying some attention to me instead of cruising your broken heart all over the Maghreb you would have known. You just didn't notice. Because you weren't interested.'

A boy ran down the balcony after a ball, breaking my fantasy.

In Egypt, twins turn into cats at night and go out to find food. If anyone beats them or throws stones at them they tell their parents the next morning and the parents remonstrate. Everyone accepts it. If you kill a cat it is terrible, because it might be someone's child. You grow out of it when you're about eleven. It explains why there are so many more cats about at night, too.

But we're not twins anyway.

No, Janie. I'll be responsible for your death if you like but I won't be responsible for your life. I couldn't have known, and the reason I couldn't is because you covered up and you lied to me, and to Mum and Dad, very efficiently and very effectively. I'm not making up with you now by accepting all the blame.

And there's no other way to make up. I cried a little. And while I was about it I thought it would be a good time to admit that this was what Harry thought I had known about all along. I disgusted him, and he hated me, because he thought I condoned Janie's prostitution, and so I cried some more to think how far he had fallen, and how hypocritical he had become, that eight years ago he had deserted me because I had told him that I was not my sister's keeper, and now he was running boy to a crook.

FOURTEEN

Unsettling

On Monday I finished reading the book – a collection of western women's writings about what used to be called the Orient, i.e. the Middle East. It was rather good, actually. Cooper rang four times, Eddie three and Harry twice. Is that the order in which they mind about me? Fear comes first, then lust, then anger?

On Tuesday the social worker came. I must say it was very prompt, once they got going. Neil said they don't like to keep things hanging around, because they realize how unsettling it is. Unsettling seems to be a really useful concept in this world. I shall keep it up my sleeve at all times.

I haven't been judged since my last exams, and that was only my knowledge of Etruscan social constructs and the various natures of pantheism. I didn't like it then either.

She was a long, intense woman with curly dark hair so limp that it couldn't get round to curling till it was down by her chin. Her eyes were buggy and water-filled, too big and too round and too pale. Her skin was waxy and her nose was sharp and I found it very hard that she was here to judge and report on whether Lily and I should be allowed to live together. Her name was Laetitia Bailey. Be nice to her, they have a lot of power.

Her manner wasn't actually that bad. There was something slightly apologetic about it, which I liked. So you damn well should apologize, coming into my home to have opinions about me.

I tidied up before she came. The place needed it anyway . . . things have been slipping around here. But I did think about it. Would it mean I was being dishonest, trying to make myself look tidier and better-ordered than I am? Would it mean I was kowtowing, playing along, sucking up? Would it mean admitting, which comes very hard to me, that I give a damn what she thinks? Well, of course I care what she thinks, because she's going to write it down and tell the judge. But I have never cared what people think. Most people anyway. But I like to know what they think, and on occasions influence what they think.

Anyway, I took Eddie's flowers round to Brigid's, because I thought they didn't really set the right tone. I wouldn't want her thinking I had men friends. Like in the Agatha Christies: unless the neighbours could say, 'She was a very nice girl and had no men friends', then your reputation is shot. Oh, dear, trying to salvage my reputation at my age. What if Ben turned up, miserable and threatening again? Or Eddie, back from Paris? I had no idea when he'd be back. Or Harry, indeed, but I think not. Next time I see Harry I shall probably be lounging naked, bound hand and foot, in Eddie's Jacuzzi full of asses' milk and Harry will be serving the champagne with a white cloth over his arm.

I wished I could meet her out somewhere. But then that's not the point, is it? The place still smelt nice from the flowers, though.

I bought a spray thing of disinfectant and sprayed half of it down the sink so that it would look like I used it all the time. Then by the time I'd cleaned the bathroom and the kitchen floor and hoovered everywhere and wiped the window sills and the windows and plumped up the cushions and washed up and hung out the laundry, Lily hated me because I'd been paying her no attention except when I'd tried to brush her hair, and we both hated the social worker because she was ruining our lives. So then I said all right, let's do some potato prints, and then I had to find an old potato print picture to stick on the wall because I didn't want Laetitia thinking we were only doing it to impress her, and I couldn't put up a new one because it would still be wet and she would notice the several layers of my double dealings.

In the end we got into the potato printing and were having a lovely time when she arrived, giggling away over what was meant to be a princess but looked more like an umbrella blown inside out. The kitchen was a mess again but it was a clean, constructive mess. Laetitia, when she entered, did not sniff at it. I, however, sniffed at her. 'Be calm, be nice, be calm,' I told myself. I hadn't told Lily who she was or what she was there for. She didn't seem bothered.

In the end, although I couldn't stop thinking, 'Please like my kitchen. If you like my kitchen perhaps I can keep my child,' it was all right. She told me she hated this part of her job because it made her feel like an estate agent (I bet she said that to all the parents). I couldn't tell half the time if she was doing small talk or intrusive questioning ('What do you do for a living, then?'), but I suppose she asked nothing that I wouldn't have wanted to know in her position. She told me she knew the school, and had spoken to Holly Brownlow who runs it. She told me she knew our doctor, and had spoken to her too. I didn't ask her what they said and she could see me not asking. She just said, before she went: 'You know better than anybody whether you're doing a good job.'

*

That night Harry called round.

I couldn't remember our last meeting, or what terms we were meant to be on. It was last Friday, when he'd driven me home from Eddie's. And before that, it was the lunch I'd walked out of. So, no, we weren't on good terms. Funny. So close below my mistrust and my despisal was a great bedrock of familiarity with him. I kicked it, and stubbed my toe. And this man thought that I'd known about Janie all along, and that I'd approved.

'Hello,' I said.

'Hello,' he said.

We waited.

'I imagine we should talk,' he said.

I imagined that, yes, we should, so I took him in and gave him a nice little shot of freezing vodka in a blue and gold Moroccan tea glass. He downed it in one.

'I'm not going to bother you,' he said, quite coldly, 'and I know you're a grown woman and make up your own mind and so on, but . . .'

Why do they keep making speeches at me? Is it the only way they can communicate?

'I am asking you as a favour, if you ever had any respect for me or faith in me, remember that, and take my advice, just don't get involved with him.'

'You're involved with him,' I said flatly.

'I'm not you.'

I laughed. 'Even Lily doesn't fall for that one.'

He lit a cigarette and the smoke curled around his face.

'Please don't smoke in here. It's bad for her skin.'

He took a long drag, then looked around for an ashtray. I took the fag off him and drowned it under the tap and binned it. For a second my hand burned where it touched his and I drowned that too.

'For her sake don't be involved with him. And for your own. Please don't be proud, please just listen.'

'But you're not telling me anything. You're just saying he's not a very nice man.'

'And he's not. Can't that be enough for you? Don't do it just to get at me, Angel, please . . .'

'I'm not doing it just to get at you! Don't flatter yourself! Why should I want to get at you?' I seemed to have forgotten that I wasn't doing it, period. So obviously I was pretending to do it, and for what other reason than to get at him? I pretended I hadn't noticed. 'And, please, stop making speeches and telling me what to do all the time.'

'I don't tell you what to do the whole time.'

'Only because we've hardly seen each other – but now you're here, what are you doing but once again telling me that I have to be good, and – actually – not do anything that *you* think is to do with sex and therefore that *you* disapprove of?'

'That's not what it's about.'

'Yes it is,' I said, forgetting that I knew that it wasn't. This was a fight I wanted to have anyway. 'If you're jealous of Eddie then you should say so and not come here full of secrets, and if you were jealous of all those men who watched me dancing you should have said so and not virtually accused me of being a stripper and a whore, and if you want me back you should just admit it to yourself.'

'I never said you were a stripper.'

'"Whichever way you shake it it's the same damn thing." I quote. You thought that what I did – my dancing, the thing I loved, because I loved it, for me – was just a sex game for men to get off on because you couldn't see any further than your own damn male nose, you didn't understand that some female things which men find sexy are not only there to be sexy for men. If we're pretty we're not just pretty for you! We're just pretty! Our legs are for walking on, our tits are for feeding babies, we sit on our arses. But you think it's all for you.'

'No I don't.'

'You plural. Sorry. I don't mean to load all the sins of all men on to you individually. But you thought my dancing was the same . . . the same school as being a whore. You did. You said so.'

'I don't know what to do about this,' he said. 'I just . . .'

'You're just still being blind, or you're refusing to talk to me or refusing to tell me why you can't or not admitting things.'

'I want to,' he said.

'But you can't, because you'd have to kill me,' I said. 'I know. I tell you what we can talk about. Let's talk about Janie. That's another thing that's been sitting between us like a brick wall for the past ten years. Tell me about Janie. Come on. You know everything. You know best. Tell me about how my sister became a whore.'

'Evangeline! Jesus Christ, after all this . . . the woman's dead, can't you leave it alone now?'

'I've left it alone for years,' I said. 'Now I'd like to know some things. Like, when did it start?'

'I don't believe this,' he said.

'And how did it work? Where did she go? Who were her clients? You know, I bet you know. Tell me.'

'What are you doing, testing me?' he said. 'I knew as little as possible about it, it was not exactly my idea of a good idea, and I'm damned if I'm going to dig it all up now.'

'Not you digging,' I said shortly.

'Well, stop it. Just bloody stop it.' He got up. 'Talk to your bloody boyfriend if you're so desperate to go on about it. And look after your kid properly. Why was that woman leaving her with me when she hardly knows me? I could have been anybody.'

That was cruel. Harry's face lends itself to cruelty sometimes. I hated him.

'Well, what were you doing here anyway?'

'I'd come to see you. As people do. You know. Visit their friends.'

Brigid was knocking on the door.

I let her in. Birnam wood was in her arms.

'Brought back your bouquet,' she said. 'Hello, Harry. They were making Caitlin sneeze.'

Harry looked at the flowers. He reached his long arm out to turn the card, and scarcely bothered to read it. With his other hand he picked up his cigarettes, and then he turned away.

'I'm not losing my temper and I'm not giving up,' he said. 'But, please, Evangeline, if you have any sense stop this. Please.' And he left.

The silence hung behind him for a moment.

'Wow,' said Brigid, impressed. 'Jealous or what! What a lot of activity all of a sudden.'

'It's not like that,' I said.

Then I sat her down and told her everything that had happened, from getting drunk with Neil to finding out about Janie, leaving nothing out. It took about an hour. I answered her questions and at the end felt both unburdened, and newly aware of exactly how large and complex a burden mine was. Brigid, however, got hold of completely the wrong end of the stick. Sometimes you wonder about people.

'Well, he's got your best interests at heart,' she said.

'What?'

'He doesn't want you walking out with a villain.'

'Who?'

'Harry.'

'But Harry works for him!'

'So he's got higher hopes for you than for himself. That's honourable.'

'But he won't tell me *why* I shouldn't be seeing Eddie, will he?'

'Does he know that you know the fellow's a villain? I don't believe he does. He doesn't want you to know. Probably doesn't want you to know that he's a villain himself. He wants you to see him in a good light. I'd say you've a good chance there.'

'What?'

'With Harry.'

I stared at her.

'Brigid! This isn't marriage guidance! All I want is to

get out of this obligation to Ben Cooper so that I can concentrate on getting rid of Jim's claim on Lily. I'm being blackmailed!'

'Well, best get him what he wants, then.'

'You mean, go back to that pyromaniac lunatic and let him rape me in the hope that I might find something – but no one will tell me what – that will get Cooper off my back and stop him from telling Jim everything?'

'Either that, or hang around a little until the situation changes. Things always change, you know. But I'd go back to Eddie if I were you. You're much better at dealing with pyromaniac lunatics than you are at hanging around. Anyway, what's a fuck?'

'Brigid!'

'Only joking,' she said.

I asked her if I could nip round and look at Janie's videos on her machine. I wasn't going to be watching them, just seeing what was on them. It shouldn't take long.

'Go round there now,' she offered. 'Maireadh's back at Reuben's so there's only Aisling and she'll be studying. I'll mind Lily.'

I didn't need to tell her to make herself at home.

*

Aisling was reading up on horse nutrition in the sitting room. The children were all asleep. The whole flat seemed to breathe with them. I looked in on them: the boys sprawled in their super-hero pyjamas, skinny chests and cropped hair, freckles on their otherwise blue-Irish skin. It's the only time you see them stationary. You could almost hear the hum of them recharging so they could spend the next day clinging like monkeys upside down from the door jamb, or being Ryan Giggs. Come to think of it, Michael seemed to be wearing a Manchester United away kit replica. 'What's wrong with QPR, Shepherd's Bush Boy?' I whispered in his ear. He shook his head as if I were a fly. It hasn't been the same for anyone since Les Ferdinand went.

Aisling said she was going to have a bath anyway. I got her to set up the video for me before she went.

*

I put on the birthday tape first, winding back to the beginning. There were no credits, just the little three-quarter circle of a clock counting down to the start, then some fizzing and squiggling on the screen, then music. Arab music. Then a belly dancer appeared, cabaret-style, westernized, in a club I didn't recognize. I didn't know her. She wasn't bad. A bit obvious, very cabaret. I fast forwarded.

Another dancer appeared. It was me. My first thought was that the date must be wrong, because I hadn't been around then. My second was that I was better than the first girl. My third was that I didn't recall the film being taken.

I tried to date it from my costume, my moves, how I looked. It was before I travelled, that was all I could make out. The setting could have been anywhere. Some restaurant.

It was interesting to watch my face. I was clearly very happy, very calm. I missed that, that happy dancing calm.

When I finished dancing there was a little glitch on the tape, a sort of blip, giving the impression it was home-made and badly edited. Then there was another dancer. Bad, very cheap. Then there were two dancers together doing some very tacky pseudo-lesbo stuff. I fast forwarded, and bent to my bag for a cigarette. I lit it, and clicked to play again. There were two girls in pathetic harem outfits, their tits out, rolling around on a couch together. One was Noor. The other girl's face was hidden in her thighs, and Noor turned a sickly vamp grin to the camera, and licked her thin lips. She was lying back and wriggling her shoulders – half a dance move, half an attempt to convey paroxysms of lustful pleasure. She didn't seem to know what she was doing.

I stopped the video and stared at her poor grin, and smoked.

The next section was a version of the dance of Salome, with almost gynaecological close-ups; the next was a girl in a *burka* – the beak-like mask of total *hajib* – masturbating in a bath. At least the shape of it was a *burka;* the sequins were more vaudeville. The next was a woman in a *chador* – the great black cape that entirely enfolds Iranian and Saudi women, scalp to toe. She didn't look Iranian. Or Saudi. As she wriggled and postured her way out of it, it became apparent she was naked underneath, unless you count an electric vibrator.

I stopped the video and lit another cigarette. Presumably it was some tool of Janie's trade. This is what prostitution involves, no doubt. No need to be surprised. Look! Janie lies and puts footage of me dancing in her pornographic compilation tapes. Janie doesn't give a fuck! Janie has no respect for me; in fact, I'm the only person who thought there was anything other than titillation in my dancing, my joy, my pleasure, my work. I don't want to get on a high horse about my dignity, but, Jesus! My lover and my sister. How marvellous to find out after ten years that no one was with you after all.

And poor pathetic Noor.

They're both dead.

I shook myself from the miasma.

What I didn't like was the trappings. All the fake Islamic stuff. Why do that with a *chador* and a *burka*? To thrill errant Muslims. And what else? To pander to that hypocrisy, to those men who still treat female entertainers as the direct descendants of the slaves and *ghawazee* of yesteryear, there to be exploited sexually. I'd met enough of those men, over the years. Muslims who felt that they had sanction from their religion. Christians with their Marys and Magdalenes. That's what you get. If you're free, you must be easy. If your feet are muddy, they assume you've been to the waterhole. Why should I imagine that just because I was different I should appear different? That anyone could tell the difference? That anyone was even looking? Even her?

And of course it would thrill western men who got off on Islamic stuff. Like Eddie.

When I thought about the men, men I knew or had met, who might have seen this tape, my skin quivered.

For a moment I recalled Zeinab and her friends dancing at home: the night before her wedding, the *leila el-henna*, or at Hassan's *sobou*, the seventh day after his birth. 'I danced all my boys to life,' Zeinab said. I've never seen anything more pure and beautiful and inspiring than the women dancing at home, for themselves, for the pleasure and the elevation of their hearts, dancing like a horse runs, like a lark sings, like a stream flows, like a mountain sits. Because it is right for you to do it. Not like this.

I put on another tape. Fast forwarded all through. More of the same. Then another, then another. Then another. The sixth tape was of even worse quality, and had even worse contents: films of people at it, out of focus, taken from one angle only, unintelligible fumblings, scrawny arses, half-visible faces, bored female ones squashed into pillows, male ones with their eyes shut yet desperate. Nasty sheets with floral patterns – the same sheets – and a duvet cover, brown on one side, pale blue on the other. It wasn't Janie's pretty girly bedroom, with its books and photos in silver frames. She wasn't any of the pasty limbs either. Different people, different girls, different men. Loveless, careless, desperate, bad sex. The people doing this did not know they were being watched.

I had by this time perfected a method of half-looking as

the stuff span by on double speed. I wanted to see what it was, I didn't want to see it. Half-watching, warning each nasty image not to think it was going to be able to stay in my mind. I had to see what there was in order to know . . .

And then out of the jerky flurry appeared Ben Cooper's face. And there was his arse – presumably Ben Cooper's arse – pounding. I wound back and stopped. Ben Cooper's twisted-up red face, in his moment of crisis. And Noor, beneath him, looking bored.

So everybody has their little bit of insurance, and this was Janie's. Ben couldn't know that this existed. He certainly didn't know it was being filmed. Couldn't have. He's a vain man, as well as a man with a well-developed sense of self-preservation – at least he used to have. And this was years ago. When Noor was alive.

I couldn't remember when she died.

Perhaps he did know about this film. Janie could have told him. Perhaps this is something he wants. Why, after all, of all the straws which must be available to a man in his line of work, did he clutch at me? Perhaps that was personal too. Perhaps he thought I had this film and that I would produce it to get him off my back. Perhaps he thought Eddie had it – though why would Eddie have it?

I turned back to the job in hand. Fast forwarded the rest of tape six. It made the edges of my stomach curl up, but at least it was short.

Tape seven started a lot easier, in a way. There was I, dancing again. It was much later, and I was much improved, doing things I had learnt in Egypt and Turkey. I was wearing an outfit that the little girls in Luxor had embroidered when I was staying with Abu Nil and Hakkim, when Nadia was ill . . . It was one of the best I ever had, crimson and silver with fringes of beads that you could make shiver like a swarm of bees – or not, which was the key. This was a more professional-looking production. I was in a club – maybe Shiraz, it was hard to tell – and the crowd were keen, mostly Levantine. There were different angles, so presumably more than one camera. Again I had no recollection of the film being made. Then the lighting changed, grew a little dimmer, and the camera drew in closer. I was dancing incredibly badly. It looked like me but could hardly have been. Then I was taking my costume off, bit by bit – that same costume – then I was writhing on the floor with my bare arse in the air and my legs akimbo. It wasn't me. It was Janie.

FIFTEEN

Eddie Again

On Wednesday the tape ran out on the answering machine, and I decided to take it as a message from God to start talking to people again.

First I rang Cooper and told him that I would do as he wanted, and on his own head be it. I was lying.

Then I rang Neil, who told me that the hearing had been fixed for next week, and that Jim's lawyers had rung him saying that Jim wanted to come and see Lily this week.

'Why didn't he just ring me?' I asked.

'Some people let lawyers go to their heads,' said Neil. 'Once they've got one, they have to get them to do everything. It makes them feel grand. Costs them, too, of course.'

Then I rang Jim, and was incredibly sweet and nice. We arranged that he would come the next day, Thursday. Nora would be at work so wouldn't be able to make it.

Then I rang Neil back and told him that Nora couldn't be bothered to take half an hour off work to see the child she was wanting to take away from a happy secure home. 'Goody,' said Neil.

Then I rang Brigid and asked her to pick Lily up from school, and invited her and the boys and Caitlin and any of the sisters who were around to tea on Thursday.

Then I rang the school and left a message for Lily that Brigid would be picking her up today.

Then I rang Mum to tell her about the hearing and she said Neil had rung her already. She wanted to read me her affidavit out over the telephone, said Dad's was brilliant, and only a paragraph long, and reminded me to put into mine about my lack of a sex-life, presuming, she said, that . . . ? She left the question hanging. So did I.

Then I rang Zeinab and we had a gossip. Her boy Hassan had got chicken pox.

Then I rang Brigid back and asked had her kids had chicken pox because Lily might be gestating them. Brigid said no they'd all had them, didn't I remember, they all got them at once last year, no it was the year before. I thought Janie's right, I don't notice what goes on in my friends' lives. Then I remembered that Janie never said that, it had just been me fantasizing an argument with her in my head. So obviously it's me that thinks it.

For a moment I seemed to get away with it. For a moment I thought of her, without my new knowledge of her slashing across the thought like a knife at ritual slaughter. But only for a moment. I'd lain awake half the night trying not to think about it, watching the shadows change shape in the room, and wishing Lily would wake up and come in to me. The other half I spent trying to fantasize more arguments with Janie. I shouted at her, I cajoled, I ignored, I pleaded, I was gentle, I was quiet, I was cold, I was kind, I was businesslike, I wept . . . she said not a word.

In daylight, I knew that she was the only person I ever would talk about it to, so I had better get used to having no answers.

Then I rang Harry and left a message saying that I was sorry that it had come to this, but that I was actually doing everything for the best as far as I could judge it. I'm not sure why I did that.

Then I decided that all these were delaying tactics: I went down to the Winfield, smoked three cigarettes, drank two large vodkas, and rang Eddie on the pay-phone.

Siao Yen answered.

'May I speak to Eddie, please?'

'How?'

'Please may I speak to Eddie?'

'Is?'

'This is Angeline Gower. Please may I speak to Eddie Bates?'

Liam's head shot up behind the bar. He glanced at me, relinquished the glasses he'd been unpacking from the dishwasher, pulled himself up and sat himself slowly down on his stool across the bar from me.

'I'm listening to this,' he said. He didn't look at all happy.

Eddie wasn't there. 'Thanks, tell him I called,' I said and hung up.

Liam looked at me.

'Well?' I said.

'Just thinking what funny company you're keeping these days,' he said.

'I can't help it,' I said. 'They're keeping me.'

He kept looking, then gave a little huff.

'Anything I can do,' he said, phrasing it as a general offer, not a specific inquiry.

'Thanks,' I said, and went home.

*

He called within the hour. Was I free? The exhibition at the Academy?

As it would be daylight and a public place, and because a daytime appointment now would keep things ticking over for a day or two, and buy me off having to tell him I would rather eat scorpions than meet him for an evening date, or in private, I said yes.

He'd pick me up, he said. No, no, said I, I had some things to do and I would meet him there. Two o'clock. Of course.

I suspected, from our previous encounter, that things had got beyond the stage where what I wore could either enflame or douse his desires. He wanted me on principle and out of pique as much as anything, and a carefully unattractive outfit could perfectly well turn out to be as inflammatory as Janie's black bustier. Who knows. I once knew a man who went into palpitations at the mere mention of grubby white bra straps. I decided not to change at all, and went out in a pair of baggy, faded, once-glamorous Indian pyjamas that would normally never get beyond the front door, let alone as far as Piccadilly.

Eddie was waiting for me in the foyer at the Academy. He looked, if I were to view him dispassionately, handsome.

Janie would have said that's only to be expected. Excitement spreads. Once things start happening, all sorts of other things start happening, even irrelevant and unwelcome ones. She would have said: so, he's handsome – of course you notice, you're all upset and therefore open to things.

Or at least . . .

Enough. Not now.

Do not imagine that I am saying I found Eddie attractive. Just that there was just enough there – just the acknowledgement, if you like, woman to man, that he could be attractive – to make his desires not quite so absurd as they might have seemed. He *could* have been a contender, if he hadn't been a dangerous madman. To which Janie would say: 'Dangerous madmen usually are rather attractive, I find.' At which point I would roll my eyes, and she would laugh, and I would laugh, and Harry would come in and say: 'What are you two on about?' Or Jim would come in and say: 'Knock it off, would you, I'm trying to concentrate in here.' He'd be watching the boxing on TV. Back then. Back then.

He greeted me lavishly. Kisses both cheeks, arm around waist, hug to body, hand on the back of the head to press me to his chest.

He was perfect company for an exhibition: erudite, if not in this field, enthusiastic, appreciative. He asked questions, followed the answers, bought the catalogue (£25 – the big beautiful illustrated one), laughed when I made jokes, which I did, and took me to Fortnum's afterwards for ice-cream. He didn't mention Cooper, Harry, the address book, his lunatic behaviour when I had last met him, his designs on my body or anything else unpleasant. I felt flattered, spoiled, and thoroughly on edge.

As we left Fortnum's I started to make going-home noises, but he tucked my arm through his and, in keeping with my 'if I stay passive perhaps we can just tick along nicely until it's all over without anything horrible happening' approach, I let him. He took me into St James's Square and started to put me into a dark green Jaguar. 'I'll take you home,' he said. Bad idea, bad idea, bad idea.

'I've still got some things to do,' I said. 'Just drop me at . . .' Still making polite excuses, courtesy still pinioning me as headlights do a rabbit.

'Of course,' he said. 'Of course,' still holding the door.

I knew suddenly what it was. It was the holding the door for me that told me. He was just being nice to me. Patient. Putting me at my ease. Off my guard. It's just like how young men used to behave when they thought you might still be a virgin. Approach her gently, indirectly, do nothing to startle her. Send flowers, take her on easy, unthreatening daytime dates, give her treats, flatter her. Drive her home, don't try to snog her on the doorstep. Ring when you say you will. Then, when she trusts you, pounce.

Well, that was all right, then. Now I knew.

Now, how can I find out how long this stage, this role, will last, and milk it?

How funny that he wants *me* to trust *him*, when here am I worried about whether he will trust me. Or rather, here's Ben worrying about that. Me, I'm just ticking over. Brigid was wrong. Me, I'd rather watch reruns of *Baywatch* on a loop tape than have anything to do with this man. I don't know when I had decided that he was connected with Janie's tapes, but decide it I had. He had to be.

Bates must really have absolutely no fear about anything Ben can do to him. Funny attitude to the police, in a criminal. Perhaps he has friends in high places.

Just ticking over.

As I relaxed into my judgement of the situation, Eddie grabbed my hair, pulled my head back, forced my jaw with his other hand and shoved something into my mouth. I started to yell, to struggle, but he yanked my head again so I was staring into his face.

'Think about Lily,' he said, quite quietly, and pushed me into the car.

*

I woke up in a room I'd never seen. The light told me it was late afternoon. My head was bad – woozy, disobedient. I shook it, which made it worse. I was lying down, on something which smelt expensive. Open, my eyes hurt. I closed them again.

I tried to think. I think I tried to think. It didn't work anyway.

*

When I woke again it was dusk. My head felt no better but something in me did.

There must be a window. It was normal yellow and purple London dusk. I imagined I must be at Pelham Crescent.

Where was the window?

Trying to move, I realized that my hands were tied. With something silky. I wished I felt like myself. I knew enough to remember that I would have laughed at the cliche. I didn't laugh.

How long before I am me?

*

It was like when you eat too many hash brownies and see the same person come into the room over and over again. When you smoke too much *shisha* and the walls start to melt as you lean against them. When you drink too much cider and the room spins and spins and spins and spins and spins and won't stop spinning. When it's too hot. When you spend two weeks on the same seat in a coffeeshop with a Colombian opium-eater, just keeping him company, you know, just keeping company, passing time. You do not leave that seat.

*

When I woke again I was in a nightclub. No, a restaurant. I was on a leather banquette. I could feel it sticking to my thighs through thin material. Eddie was beside me, drinking champagne and laughing. He had his arm round my shoulder but he was talking to somebody else – a man. My eyes were already open when I woke. What the hell had he given me?

Our table was covered with half-eaten food: a dish of greenish ta'amiah, babaganouk, tsatsiki, kibbeh. Damp ravaged mounds, dripping olive oil, with flags of long, sweet-leafed parsley askew atop. Castles after a battle. The droplets of water on a quartered cos lettuce gleamed at me. Long clean spring onions, shining like bone. Scarlet tomatoes. Dishes of meat, grilled, dripping a little, a little juice, a little marinade, a little blood. The plate in front of me had a knife and fork resting against it. The food was half-eaten, the taste of chargrilled meat was in my mouth.

I was wearing a loose chiffony dress with a belt at the hips. I didn't know it. I had no underwear on.

First thought through the swamp of my brain: Lily.

Lily's all right. She's with Brigid. Brigid will cover.

Jesus, it was Shiraz. It had changed, though. It was noisier, and the people were wilder. It seemed late. The same night, I supposed.

I wondered how I had been behaving. All I needed to do was carry on behaving the same way, then make a run for it. What, until Ben frightened me into coming back?

No, I'm not coming back again, I'm going to Egypt with Lily. Become Harem – outlaw. Perhaps from the same root as *Haram*, forbidden. The other possible root of the word is *H'rim* – Sanskrit for keep out. Keep out.

Keep awake. Keep thinking.

Eddie was taking no notice of me. The other men . . . I didn't know them. Arab-looking. Rich. One had a diamond ring which flashed in the low light. I couldn't make out what they were saying.

The music changed. Perhaps it was that the voices died down. Ah, yes. The dancer.

I didn't know her. Well, I wouldn't. A lot changes in three years. She was young and thin. The old ideal of a dancer is a willow stem planted in a sand dune – but not this modern girl. She had the pomegranate tits, though.

'Tits like pomegranates, eh, darling?' Eddie was talking to me. Whispering. I felt his breath. And his hand on my arse. My brain must still be addled. He just said what I was thinking. It's just drugs. Don't be frightened.

She was good. Very proud-looking. Not English – maybe Turkish. It's so hard to tell, in a club. Everyone has become so westernized, such a western version of the East. The crowd liked her. Lots of handclaps and encouragement. Eddie liked her too – beckoned her over, and she came. Fire burned up the edges of my mind, tearing up the periphery of my vision. I closed my eyes to block it and it took over the whole of me, made me quiver. Eddie held me close.

'Cold, sweetheart?' His hand crept up, rubbing my tit.

The girl vamped him, snake arms, jump and shimmy, veil round his head, emphasizing her already emphasized tits with her upper arms, pressing them together inches from his nose. I could smell her make-up, and her sweat. Sway figure eight, sway figure eight, sway figure eight. Pulse and thrust, pulse and thrust. No fertility or childbirth here, just unadulterated coitus.

'Like her?' murmured Eddie. 'Shall we take her home?' He reached for a champagne bottle and ran his fingers up and down it, looking at her, and at me.

I made an idiotic, mooney, out-of-it face for him. He brought his face close to mine and nuzzled me.

I thought you wanted to win me fair and square, break me like the plucky filly I am. I thought you were going to make me want you. Isn't drugs cheating? Wouldn't drugs make it no better than rape, which as we know doesn't interest you? Or have you given that up? Are you just going to take me any way you can?

Eddie was burrowing in my neck. The dancer was vamping both of us. I looked up at her over the fine grey hairs on the back of his neck and a flash of Arabic leapt from my mouth: '*Ouw'Ï*' – don't you dare. Even if she was Turkish, she got the message.

Eddie, one hand creeping over my thigh, under the skirt and heading for my clunge, did not.

Enough already. My body is for love and dancing, not for this crap. I tried to stand. What with Eddie, the dancer, the table and the immovable banquette it was hard. And furthermore my legs wouldn't do it. Jelly. Jelly legs, jelly head. I seemed to be fading out again.

*

When I woke again, I was naked, and Eddie was standing above me.

Oh, shit.

Again I pretended not to have woken.

He left.

My head was clearer. I was in a bedroom, an anonymous posh English guest bedroom. There were two windows, long and high, with drawn chintz curtains, and all the flouncey bits. Pelmets. There was an armchair, an unattractive carpet, flowers, two doors, a fireplace with a large mirror over it, and ornaments. I wasn't tied. By the feel of my body I had not been fucked. I stood up. My legs were OK. I looked in the mirror. Just me. Just standing there, naked, in a strange room.

I tried one of the doors. Locked. I tried the other. A bathroom. I washed, before I realized there were no towels. I went back into the bedroom and dried myself on the bedspread. Shiny chintz, no good, but better than nothing.

Eddie came in as I was drying. I stood up straight and stared at him.

'Cover yourself!' he said, shocked.

I pulled the bedspread across my front. Automatically it was a dance movement, a drawing of the veil.

'Hide those pomegranates!' he said.

My head was not clear enough to formulate a policy.

He sat on the end of the bed.

'I fucked the other girl,' he said. 'You watched, though I don't suppose you made much of it. I'm saving you up.'

So my career as his personal sex doll was beginning. But it's better than last time. Lots of people know where I would be. Brigid, Ben Cooper, Harry, Liam. I've been talking my mouth off, really.

That is presuming that I am here. Pelham Crescent.

Eddie picked up the phone and ordered some tea.

'I will be missed, you know,' I said.

'Of course,' he said.

'Doesn't it worry you?'

'Not at all. It's too late. I'm off any minute.'

'So Ben said. He said it wasn't clear where.'

'I'm off, I'm off, and all is waste and nonsense in my wake . . . Don't worry, I'll send you back. In one piece, probably.'

'Probably?'

'Meaning if you behave . . .' he said. 'Or, meaning that I have no intention of harming you but I'm not telling you so because I might want to frighten you.'

'What does behave mean?'

He gave me a louche look. 'Oh, work it out for yourself.'

'Fuck you?'

'Language!' he snapped. 'No.'

'Want to fuck you?'

'Oh, *do* - oh, *please*,' he said.

'But you've got me here under duress. How could you know if I wanted to or not?'

'I'm very vain, you know,' he said. 'I'll believe all sorts of things to my own advantage.'

I was tired. I cannot spend a year here naked playing Beauty and the Beast with him. I am not going to sleep with him. He's off any minute. So why is he wasting time? Neither in practical terms nor from the roots of his . . . attachment, can I work out what he's doing. But he can win, in his terms. Perhaps it is enough for him just to have me here before he goes. Whoops, mind the phraseology there. But *when* exactly is he saving me up for?

There was a knock on the door, and Siao Yen brought the tea in. Peppermint, in little gold and green glasses. Very Arab. Rather like my blue ones, but better quality, of course. She took no notice whatsoever of the fact I was naked, and slipped out again.

We sipped.

'Do you know how I met your sister?' he said.

'No,' I said. I got a sort of thrill out of saying it. Just saying no, about anything, about any of this mad stuff.

But of course No I don't know means, Yes – tell me. And that was all I wanted. And exactly what I wanted. To be told. And he told me.

'Our mutual friend, little Ben Cooper, took me out to see you dancing. Yes, Ben! We went to a little place somewhere north of Oxford Street, down some steps, all very secret-looking, and inside, after dinner, there was you – oh! My dream! You were wonderful. So beautiful, so proud, so gorgeous, so mobile. From the angles of your head to the meat on your arse – perfect. Every move.

'So I said to Ben, I must meet her. And he said that you were very proud, very haughty, and that you did not agree to meet men. I begged him. He said he did not think you would. I begged him and begged him. I begged him for weeks. He said he would ask. I was in heaven!

'Then he said you said no. He said you only entertained Muslims . . . Are you cold, my love?'

'No. Go on.'

'Have some more tea.'

'Thank you.'

'I went to watch you again and again. I was besotted. In love. I never approached you because I didn't want to frighten you off. I returned to Ben and said to him, "Look out the window." Outside there was a beautiful little Mercedes. I said, "That is for her. If you introduce us, there is another one, for you."

'A week later I met you . . .'

He broke off to pour more tea. 'But you're tired,' he said. 'It's nearly dawn. You should sleep.'

Don't you Scheherazade me. I looked at him. Luckily he did not have Scheherazade's patience. He couldn't resist it.

'I took you to the Ritz for dinner. You were charming. You loved the car. Without your costume and your make-up and the magical movements of your dance you were not as exciting as I had expected, but I put that down to the natural bathos of achieving the fantasy, of holding the impossible woman in my arms and seeing all too clearly the sad flaws of reality when considered against the ineffable delights of the distant and the unobtainable. Stage lighting must be very flattering, I thought. Though you were happy to fuck me, and you wore your costumes for me, you declined to dance for me. You loved the two thousand pounds I left on the bedside table. You were not worth it. I kept you for a month, after which I did not call you again.'

There are times when your body seems to pass into suspension. Now was one of them.

'Later, I saw you dance again. By chance. I had not known that you would be appearing – I was just getting cheap fixes of other girls. My dream of you had been sullied, exploded. But there you were again. You were more magical than ever. As usual, unlike most girls, you did not vamp and cajole, you did not have to beg for tips. There you were, up there, perfect woman, and there were us, down below, all the men, howling silently for you. If I could bottle the sex that you inspired! All the women were happy – they knew they would get their share that night.'

It made a sort of sense.

'But you did not know me. I stared at you; even caught your eye. You did not know me. I called to you; you did not hear me. I poured brandy at your feet, a libation to my goddess. You did not look at me. When the flame of my ardour burned up all around you, you looked my way, but you did not know me. When I offered you money, you scorned me, and looking at you I knew I had never met you, never fucked you, never bought you, never looked at your face, your own self within the uniform of your outfit and your position, and beyond the lust inspired by your timeless movements.

'The next day I cut Ben Cooper out of eighteen business ventures in which he was involved, much to his loss. I made some inquiries, and found that you had a sister – an alley cat who looked quite like you. I had not been fooled by any physical similarity, but by the gap between fantasy and life, between archetype and the tart on my arm. I found her, took up with her again – at a greatly reduced price – and learnt to enjoy her for her own qualities, which were many. I never held the trick against her. She was just a girl. Girls like her do what they're told. She was making films for Cooper – did you know that? Dirty little films – rather fun. He financed them and believed that she was marketing them – which she was, through me. He didn't know that. We never told him I had discovered his deception. She fiddled him left right and centre on those films. He made no money. Wherever I could arrange for him to lose, he lost.

'Janie was disappointed in him. She thought me cleverer and more fun! She was right. And she never liked sleeping with him. She wanted me to take her on, and a few of Ben's other girls too. So I did. I employed her boy Jim in one of my companies, to keep things tidy. Jim was not a problem, to her or anybody. Jim is not clever.

'Do you know I only took Harry on because of you? A vague, undying, sentimental notion that he connected me to you . . . otherwise I don't think I would have taken him. I don't like him. He's a smartypants. Always seems to know something.

'I knew when you went away, of course. I always hoped you would come back.

'Janie's pregnancy was not convenient, of course, but it didn't matter because by then she was less in the field, as it were, and more behind the scenes. She had given up that little job she had. I knew she never told you anything. I never told her anything about you, and how I felt about you – how I still feel, you know. Nothing has changed. She suspected. After our first meeting, how could she not? We even did the same ploy a few times ourselves – I tell you, you always got a very good price. But not often. We didn't want to damage your reputation.'

I believed him. I believed everything he said. How interesting it all was. How tired I was. How sick.

I pulled up the bedspread around me and lurched to the bathroom to puke. Then I went back into the bedroom and began to throw things at him: a vase, the tea glasses, a china spaniel off the mantelpiece. Then he was lying on top of me, pinning me down, his mouth all over my face, trying to hoick his dick out and get it into me. But I can wriggle . . . I can wriggle and flex like a great big fish, I can swerve and avoid and snap and entangle, I learnt my muscles from the Ouled Nail, no one man is going to pin me.

So there I was stark naked in front of the fireplace with the poker in my hand. So I clouted him.

And then . . . and this is the bit that surprises me. Seeing him lying unconscious on the unpleasant carpet, with his head flung back, his shirt collar loosened, his handsome face white and his elegant trousers open from the waist with his penis, extraordinarily still rigid – what was the blood doing there? Wasn't it needed elsewhere? – I was washed over with . . . well, it was lust, but it was something else too. I think it was joy, to have at last one of these sods that have been tormenting me at my mercy. It was glee. One moment he loves me, the next he is raping me; the next he is out cold. Well, try this, sweetheart. Try this. And don't be flattered. I don't care what you think.

So I carefully put down the poker, within reach, and quietly wrapped my naked self around him. Mine for the taking, and I had had none in so long. I couldn't keep still, just moving, moving, circling, grinding, encircling, building the heat, rubbing my breasts on his clean shirt-front, laying my mouth on his neck, finding his cock – How extraordinary! I must ask a doctor about this – he was out cold, but it was game. Shapely, large, rockhard, and all mine. And just playing with it, putting it in various places, as I liked, places that hadn't felt flesh in too long, all those lonely empty neglected bits of body, armpits and toes and hands and teeth and hair. And I kissed him a lot and stroked him and scratched him and fed my pomegranates to his immobile mouth, and amused myself no end before taking him into me by pure hunger and suction.

I did him. I did him proper. He hardly stirred. Four years of repressed woman; a fabulous dance. And he missed it. He joined in a little – twitchings and stirrings, little moans. Well might he moan. It didn't bother me. I was having a *marvellous* time. Occasionally it seemed as if he might be going to come – but he didn't. I didn't let him.

And when I was finished I wiped myself on his hands, and found myself starting over again, and then on his shirt-tails, to make sure he knew what had been going on without him.

SIXTEEN

Out

I hurtled down the stairs like a banshee, flinging open doors as I went to see if there were any exits or any clothes. The house was old, and a weird shape – corridors off, extra staircases. I was way up high, that much I could tell. But as to what was a bedroom, or a way out . . . that I couldn't. I headed down.

Two flights down Siao Yen was there on a landing. She was little. I could barge straight through her, knock her sideways, so long as she wasn't a secret expert in some diabolic Oriental martial art. But she stood aside, and said as I passed: 'He deserved it. If you need a witness, I'll say whatever you want. Poor old Buenos Aires will have to do without him now!'

I gave a glancing stare backwards as I hurtled, and decided I was hallucinating. Down, down, down.

I came to a kitchen. Too far. Hanging on the door was a flowered housecoat, Siao Yen size. I put it on, pulled it round me, but it gaped. There was an apron, too. That covered the front. I pulled open the nearest door – some kind of pantry. The next was a broom cupboard. The next was a huge dark glass-roofed and glass-walled room. I could see sky and stars, above me and below. I was almost in the swimming pool before I realized what it was. I slammed the kitchen fire extinguisher out through one of the glass sheets of wall and I was out, in a garden, wet grass beneath my feet, and the smell of an English summer night in my nostrils.

Well, I'm not in Pelham Crescent.

I ricocheted around the garden for a minute or two before I realized that without taking stock I would end up in a cowfield. I stopped, panting, hurting. Apart from me, all was silent and calm. It was so beautiful that I lay down on my back and breathed nicotiana and night-scented stock. In to four, hold for two, out to eight. Beautiful. I was laughing. Sex, my God! I must do it some more. Maybe that's what men are. Battery rechargers. Plug yourself in and watch your energy levels go wild. Poor fucker.

Sitting up and looking around, I saw the shape of the house defined by the moonlight emerging around it. I was in a back garden, and the darkness round beside the house seemed to lead to the front. Jumping up, I followed the smooth wet lawn, treading daisies between my toes. Sure enough it led to a driveway, lined by mounded rockery, saxifrage glowing in the huge light of the suddenly visible moon. Standing in the driveway, gleaming in the moonlight, was the Pontiac. It looked like a ghost. It was a ghost. My car from the past, waiting for me, just where I would want it to be. What the hell was it doing there?

Is Harry here, then?

Time to go. Even more so.

I walked over, gravel crunching my feet as the daisies had soothed them. The door was unlocked, the keys in the ignition.

From way up, up the house I heard a noise – a bump, and a voice. So he wasn't dead. Probably just as well. I don't kill people, heck no. My methods are far more subtle. He tried to rape me, so I fucked him in revenge.

Unless it was Harry. But I hadn't heard the car draw up. How long had he been here? What was he doing?

Definitely time to go.

I jumped in my car, and followed my nose.

*

By the time I could work out where I was, the dawn was well up and my nose seemed to have led me to the outskirts of Milton Keynes. Not so bad. I criss-crossed a million mini-roundabouts until I found the London road and turned into a Happy Eater. Nobody seemed to find my dress that outlandish. Clearly Happy Eaters at dawn are the place to be. Trusting to Harry's old habit of keeping a fiver or two tucked somewhere unlikely in case of emergencies, I found a fifty pound note, slightly the worse for wear, down the back of the back seat. Egg bacon sausage chips beans and two slices, with tea, gave me change for the phone. Before I could call I puked it up again. In the loo I realized that the reason my feet were still wet was because one of them was bleeding. I washed them and bound them up in paper hand towels, which disintegrated.

I looked no more unseemly with the housecoat sleeves ripped off and wrapped around my feet. One was bad, the other not. I could drive one-footed.

It was ten to seven. I rang Brigid. Maireadh answered. I could picture her, dopey on the sofa, groping in her sleep for the telephone, just to stop the damn noise.

'Maireadh,' I said. 'How's Lily? Listen, I've had a bit of an adventure but I'll be along soon, tell Brigid everything's all right, and tell Lily I'll be picking her up later and tell her I'm sorry I wasn't there last night and tell Brigid I don't know what I'd do and I'm sorry, I'm really sorry, and if she could get Lily to school and say thank you to her, I'm sorry to wake you . . .' and then I went and was sick again, and then I sat in the car and cried for ten minutes, then I dozed for ten minutes, then I went in and had a black coffee, then I filled up with petrol and then I turned on Harry's tape machine in my car. It was Bob Marley. I wound on the tape till I found the one about the three little birds on my window saying every little thing's gonna be all right, and I believed every word.

Janie always felt cheated. Always felt that the parents in educating us had cut us off from what we were and set us up as something we could never be. She always had wanted something else. She always had been willing to blame others for the fact that she didn't have what she felt was hers. I just never knew it was so personal. I never knew she was jealous of my dancing. I used to give her things all the time when I was making all that money when I was a teenager. I never thought she minded. Stealing my dancing, stealing my reputation, stealing the likeness of me, stealing my sex and flogging it. And I never noticed, never helped.

I'd use her money to pay Neil.

That wouldn't take all of it.

Can money be tainted?

If Noor's family had ever treated her decently I'd send some to them.

So, what? Found a home for repentant whores? The Janie Gower Redemption Centre? Or for the female victims of Islamic fundamentalists? Or a brothel for women, with Eddie and Ben as the star attractions . . . but who would ever pay to sleep with Ben Cooper? Ha ha Eddie. For a second I was tempted to go back and do it again. Oh, he was good. He was unconscious, but he was *good*. I kept laughing. I'd had no idea I had that kind of pervy sexuality going on inside me. Good morning, my body! How nice to see you again! We must see more of each other!

I just didn't feel like using the money to feed and educate Lily.

Then I got another coffee. Then I drove home.

*

Well, almost home. I stopped off at Zeinab's. She was digging and fossicking in the garden, with a big skirt hitched up around her knees and a big hat on her head. Her boys were gambolling around her, baffing at each other like puppies.

'Why aren't they at school?' I asked, as I greeted them.

'Chicken pox,' she said. 'I told you.'

Oh, God, I'm a shit friend.

'Not like you to forget something like that,' she said. 'You look terrible. What are you wearing? Come and have a coffee.'

Lovely warm milky coffee, made by a friend, given by a friend. The boys looked disgustingly well. 'It's an extra holiday for them,' she said. 'They are hardly itching. They want chicken pox for ever.'

I was so happy, so quiet, so ordinary, I almost forgot what I'd come for.

'Zeinab,' I said. 'Can we come and stay for a few days? Lily and me? There's something that needs to blow over.'

'Of course,' she said. She asked no questions and I told her nothing. She said did I want to sleep for a bit now. I said no, but that I would gladly borrow some clothes.

'Anything you need,' she said. God bless her.

'I'll be back in an hour or two,' I said, and drove home in a beautiful linen *gallabeya*, my feet bandaged, clutching the housecoat and apron and bloodstained sleeves in a plastic bag.

*

At home the machine was flashing away.

Mum: Where was I, could I give her a ring?

Dad: Where was I, could I give him a ring?

Neil: Where was I, could I give him a ring?

Cooper: Where was I, could I give him a ring?

Cooper again: Where was I? There was no point trying to avoid him.

Laetitia the social worker: she wanted to see us again, would it be all right if she came on Thursday afternoon, was she right in thinking that Lily wasn't at school then, could I call her back if it's not OK, otherwise she'll just come.

Shit. Today is Thursday. Today is when Jim is coming.

Last was a message from Harry: if I got this presumably I was back: I was to leave again immediately and go and stay with a girlfriend or something, not my parents, and call him as soon as I was elsewhere, not now, just go. Please he said.

Oh, I thought.

It had of course crossed my mind to wonder why Harry's own runabout had been handily sitting there in Bates's drive with the keys in the ignition. It was just that my mind hadn't been in a fit state to notice what was crossing it that morning. Was he still at Eddie's?

Well, my plan was to go away anyway.

Shit. My handbag was still . . . wherever.

But my address book was on my desk. I grabbed it, some clothes, some for Lily, and her eczema creams, and shoved them in a bag. Then I used the spare key to double lock everything I could think of to double lock and went out to the Pontiac. It had got a ticket. I laughed, and drove back to Zeinab's.

On the way I went past Lily's school, and peered through the window, where I could see her splashing her hands in a plastic tub of water. Brigid had redone her plaits. She was concentrating hard. I knew she would be humming a little song to herself, with strange words, working through things in her mind, going over all the strange and seemingly inexplicable things that happen every day in a three-year-old's life. Because a three-year-old knows so little, and learns so much, all the time. Coping away. My little sponge.

I got to Zeinab's at noon, slept for an hour, and then rang Harry.

'Where are you?' he wanted to know.

'You work for the only person that you think I need to hide from,' I said. 'Why should I tell you where I am?'

'Angel, trust me,' he said.

'Fuck off,' I said. I was very happy.

'OK,' he said. 'Does Ben know where you are?'

'No.'

'Don't tell him – don't speak to him.'

'I wasn't going to.'

'Have you got my car?'

'My car,' I said.

'Oh, for fuck . . . Where have you been?'

'None of your damn business. Having fun.'

'Do you know where Eddie is?'

'Who wants to know?'

'Angeline, are you drunk?'

'Can't tell,' I said. 'But listen . . . no, it's all right . . .'

'Angeline?'

'I am going to go away. Don't worry. It's a good idea. But Harry . . .' I said.

'Yes.'

'This afternoon I have Jim, and the social worker, and a million other people coming to tea.'

'Cancel them.'

'I have to keep my date. The woods are dark and wild and deep but I have promises to keep and miles and miles and miles and miles to go before I sleep.'

'Cancel.'

'The hearing is next week.'

'Angel . . .'

'I won't see Ben and I won't see Eddie. Not if I can help it. I'm not worried about anything else.' I didn't tell him I was worried I would fight Ben and kidnap Eddie. Hey, good idea! 'I'll try and cancel this afternoon.'

'Where are you?'

'Not telling you. Got to go and get Lily.'

I hung up.

All the mixed feelings were still there, and I just didn't care about them. All the doubt and confusion, and I didn't give a damn. Why did I spend so much time trying to pretend that everything was all right? It's not and it won't be, and it doesn't matter. Fuck it. I'm dancing in the light of the flames on the battlements, going Ha ha ha. Harry's all right. Everything is all right. I'm queen of the fucking May.

I couldn't get hold of Jim or Laetitia.

I was so sleepy. I went to get Lily. She was happy, sweet, so pleased to see me she just yelled. At four, we all went to the flat: Zeinab, the boys and us.

How *could* this whole mess fail to be noticed? It can't! Ben can ruin us . . . just like that. And then Lily and I shall go off to Buenos Aires and live happily ever after with the psychotic gangster. How *marvellous.* I must mention it to him.

SEVENTEEN

Showtime

The flat had been ransacked. Broken glass, books pulled out, furniture unravelled, my study awash with papers, and a bobby on the door. Beside him was a huge bouquet, just like the last one but half as big again. Presumably he had ordered it yesterday. I picked it up and cuddled it.

'Angeline?' said Zeinab. 'Are you loved?' I grinned at her.

'Miss Gower?' said the bobby.

'Ah, yes.' I recognized him. 'You're Liam's friend, aren't you?'

'Oh yeah,' he said, and immediately became human. 'We couldn't find you.'

'I was hiding,' I said. 'I was expecting this.' Which wasn't true.

Stupid Ben not to just do this to Bates's in the first place. It would have made everything much simpler. But then I don't have a burglar alarm, and Eddie does, rather.

'We've fingerprinted and everything. Neighbour called us. Heard a noise and saw a fellow running off. Any ideas?'

'Ben Cooper,' I said. 'Detective Superintendent, either in person or employing some other cack-handed innocent under duress.' Yes I'm sure he gave me a funny look. In exchange I gave him the name of the police station. He looked as if he knew he ought to look surprised, but wasn't.

'We'll be needing to take a statement . . . can you see if anything's missing?'

'It won't be,' I said. 'I've got nothing he wants.' The videos were still at Brigid's – even if he knew they existed. Nothing else would interest him. He didn't know I had anything anyway. Him and his off-chances. He must be desperate: raiding the straw's flat. Now if the policeman would just go, I could get on.

'Um . . . look, could you go?' I said nicely.

'Sorry?'

'I want to get tidied up. I've people coming round, including a social worker who can give evidence that my child should be taken away . . . please.'

He looked at me. 'Someone will have to take a statement,' he said.

'Later,' I said. 'Promise.'

He shrugged. 'This evening, probably,' he said. 'Any friend of Liam's,' and he wandered back down the balcony.

Zeinab was giving me a very pure look.

'I'll tell you everything. Boys! Play football. Come on, let's tidy.'

Once the worst of the mess was shoved into the study, and the study door was shut, the flat didn't look too bad. We sent Omar up the road for bread and milk, and I put Eddie's flowers – old and new – in vases all along the wall of the balcony. My feet were bleeding again.

'OK,' I said. 'Showtime.'

Brigid and Maireadh and Aisling and all were coming up the stairs. Behind them, Jim. Behind him Laetitia.

'I'm so sorry,' I said, as I let her in. 'Everybody seems to have turned up at the same time, I hope you don't mind.'

It was mayhem, all through the flat and out on to the balcony. Six small boys and two small girls, three mothers, two Irish aunties, tea and toast, a penalty shootout competition against the end wall, Birnam wood all over everywhere, Brigid trying to find out what had happened, Zeinab taking pride in not asking, me glitter-eyed and madly courteous, trying not to talk to Brigid and apologizing with horrid falsity to Jim who sat there like a poor rabbit, a lone man in the world of women, a eunuch in the den of houris. Lily took no notice of him whatsoever, and greeted everybody else with *zagareets* of delight.

Laetitia laughed and said what fun. I introduced her to Jim. He said, yes they'd met, she'd been round to see him and Nora too.

'Oooh,' I said. 'What's their place like? Do tell. Will Lily like it better than here? I don't suppose they live in a flat, do they? I know Jim's boss is a *very* wealthy man.'

'What boss?' he said.

'Oh, maybe you don't work for him any more. You know. Janie's little friend.'

Jim went white.

Bull's eye! Jim knows lots of things, but he didn't know that I knew some too.

'Tell me, Jim,' I whispered, as Maireadh took Laetitia off to get a cup of tea. 'Was it really you who used to knock her about or was it the punters? Or Bates? Or maybe Cooper?'

He'd gone all stiff. Eddie was right. He wasn't clever.

'I never hurt her,' he said at last. 'I always told you that.' It was true. He always had. I had always despised him for it.

Hassan had fallen over. I directed Zeinab to the sticking plasters.

'So you never hit her?'

'Never,' he said. 'I loved her.' As if that proved anything.

'Why did she want to run away from you the whole time, then?'

'She didn't.' He was outraged. 'She bloody didn't. I helped her. I was useful. I helped her with all sorts of things.'

'Like what?'

'When those two got mad at her, I was always there. I was the only person who knew everything. I was always kind to her . . .'

'Was she kind to you?'

Lily wanted milk. Jim stared at her. I left them together while I went to fetch her a glass, hobbling on my sore feet.

'Here you are, hon.' She wrapped herself round my legs and wouldn't be disentangled. I stroked her and picked her up and told her I loved her to bits. She kissed my nose, and then went away with Michael on a promise of chocolate biscuits Brigid had brought.

'No, she wasn't,' said Jim. 'Kind. No she fucking wasn't. She fucked everybody in sight, whether or not they paid her. Everybody. Oh, except for me, of course.'

'I'm sorry?' said Laetitia, coming back across to us.

'Fucking Janie,' he said.

'I'm sorry, am I intruding . . . ?' she said, which was quite funny coming from a social worker. 'Is there something . . . ?'

Jim stood up. The doorbell went. Lily came back with her biscuit. I felt terribly happy. Imminent relief was all around me, in the air, palpable. This bloody mess was going to shatter to smithereens, and at the end of it either life would be not worth living or I would rise triumphant and transcendent from the wreckage, with Lily glowing in my arms. Either way, I would know; I would have moved on.

'What's the matter with your feet?' said Jim.

'Angeline!' called Zeinab from the front of the flat. 'There's a man here.'

'Why'd he ring the bell? The door's open,' said Maireadh.

It was Cooper.

'Come outside,' he said.

'I can't possibly, Ben, I have guests.' I was delighted to see him. This man, a pimp and pornographer, had sold my sister's body, and masqueraded it as mine; had made a whore of me without my even knowing. The more of my sister's disgrace that was due to him the better, as far as I was concerned. And he'd ransacked my flat. And he had a nasty hairy backside and fucked with his eyes closed and a look of pain on his face. I started to laugh.

'Come,' he said.

'No,' I said.

Standoff.

'We're all friends here,' I said. 'You know Jim Guest, don't you? I believe you were his girlfriend's pimp. My daughter Lily? Go on out, darling, take the boys.' I don't want her to see everything fall apart. Not knowing where it will all land.

Zeinab started to herd the children out again.

'Go with them?' I said, and she nodded, her black eyebrows very high.

Maireadh and Brigid sat down, agog, ready to watch the fun. Laetitia was looking at me oddly, so I introduced her to Ben. Did I mention that I was mad with fatigue and pain? I was. Fatigue, pain, adrenaline, anger, and the knowledge that it can't last much longer.

'This is Laetitia Bailey. She's a social worker. She's assessing Jim and I, to see which would be the better parent for Lily. Laetitia, this is Detective Superintendent Ben Cooper. He's a policeman,' I added, unnecessarily. 'Our hearing is next week, Ben, so we're all rather busy with the case. Perhaps I could talk to you when it's over, unless of course you have something to add?'

It was so easy. I know I am in the right, I thought. Out of chaos comes clarity. *Fitna!* Beautiful woman, disaster, madness, chaos.

Ben was watching me. He didn't know what I was doing. But then he didn't know that I didn't know what I was doing either.

'Angie,' he said, cautiously.

'Don't call me Angie.'

Brigid snorted.

'If you can't behave, Brigid, you'll have to leave the room,' I called, without looking at her. She snorted again. I love that woman.

Jim had a very strange look on his face. He was starting to mutter.

'Sorry, Jim?' I said.

'What the fuck is he doing here?' he burst out. 'I'm not going to sit here with that bastard . . .'

'I don't want him here either, Jim. I don't like him either. Ben – why don't you just go away?' It occurred to me I was behaving a bit like Eddie: cheerful and mad.

'Urn . . .' said Laetitia. Maybe she has some professional skills which could be useful here. Crisis management. But I don't want it managed.

Jim was beginning to sway from side to side. He may not ever have hit Janie, but Cooper looked in for one.

Ben glanced around, then mobilized. 'Come on, Jim, don't be stupid,' he said. 'Angeline, I want to talk to you, *now*.'

Oh, such male assertion.

'Oh, blah,' I said. 'I'm not talking to you.'

It was at that point that Jim belted Ben, crying out that he'd lost everything before because of this bastard and he wasn't going to lose everything this time. Brigid and Maireadh made some loose attempts to pull him off; the rest of us stood back. Bang crash wallop.

'What did he lose last time?' asked Laetitia. I was beginning to like her – her calm interest, as if we were beetles and she was David Attenborough.

'Janie, my sister,' I whispered. 'Cooper made her a prostitute. He was her pimp, all the time Jim and she were together.'

'Oh!' she gasped.

The fight was very small and pathetic and lasted about ten seconds. Ben pushed Jim off, Jim burst into tears. The rest of us stood around and watched. How silly, how human, how much too late.

Zeinab called to me from outside in Arabic: 'There's more men coming up!'

'Eddie!' I thought.

It wasn't Eddie. Maybe it was worse, I didn't know. Four men in suits. I'd never seen them before. And Harry.

'Miss Gower,' they nodded to me, each in turn. They were like funeral attendants or something. Time to stand back. I did so, giggling. I stood with Laetitia and Brigid, and nudged them with my elbows.

'Detective Superintendent,' one of them murmured.

It was Cooper who looked aghast.

'Come along,' murmured the suit.

Cooper stood like a sack.

He wasn't saying anything. How unlike him. Silence, from Ben Cooper.

They moved round to stand two on either side of him. He looked up at me. 'Bitch,' he said. 'Just like your sister.' I stuck my tongue out at him.

Jim started yelling at him again. Harry slapped Jim's face sharply. 'Sit down,' he said.

Maireadh gave Jim a cup of tea.

'Sorry about this, Miss Gower,' said the suit, and they turned and led Ben out.

There was a silence, broken only by Jim hiccuping to himself.

Then: 'What's going on?' said Laetitia.

One of the suits stuck his head back through the door.

'Sir?' he said.

'Umm?' said Harry.

Harry?

'Leave it in your hands this end, sir?'

'Yeah,' he said.

He turned to Brigid: 'Give us a moment, please.'

Brigid and Maireadh stood up, goggling at me.

'I'll see you later,' I said. 'I'll see you later.' They went outside.

He turned to Laetitia. 'Sorry, Miss, er . . .'

'Laetitia Bailey,' I said. 'The social worker. Harry Makins.'

'Miss Bailey,' he said. 'Sorry. We had to arrest someone.

Unfortunately it had to be here. He's been attempting to blackmail Miss Gower over . . .'

Watch your mouth, Harry.

'. . . allegations about her sister's past, things which Miss Gower didn't know about. This was the only place where we knew he would come.'

'But he's a policeman,' said Laetitia.

'Yes,' said Harry.

'So are you,' I said. I was astounded.

'Yes,' said Harry. 'Have been for a while now.'

'Not in the motor trade?'

'Only when required.'

I didn't know if it was good or bad.

'Miss Bailey?' said Harry.

'It's Mrs, actually,' said Laetitia. 'Or Ms.'

'Ms. Yes, of course. Look, could we make an appointment, before the hearing, so that I can explain to you Miss Gower's involvement in all this? It would be a great shame if her being the victim of crime should count against her in this case . . .'

'Certainly,' she said.

It seemed she should go, but she didn't.

'So we'll speak, shall we?' said Harry.

'Of course,' she said. 'But if there's anything you know which is pertinent to the case . . .'

'Well, of course there is.'

'Well?'

'Oh, God,' said Harry. I was pleased that his masterful

and efficient new manner was not flawless, that he could still be inarticulate when it came down to it.

I don't know what Harry is like. I don't know who he grew up to be.

Laetitia was just looking at him kindly, willing him to talk.

'Jim,' said Harry, grasping a let-out.

'Yeah?'

'Is there anything you want to tell Ms Bailey? Now that Nora isn't here?'

Jim looked up through red eyes.

'Like what?'

'Anything about Janie?'

'I know about Janie,' said Laetitia.

'What do you know about her?' asked Harry.

'That she was . . . a prostitute.'

Harry nodded.

'Well, prostitutes have babies all the time . . . the case is certainly complicated, and in law . . .'

'Does it suggest anything obvious?' he said.

She looked blankly at him.

He stared back, his green eyes steady. 'Don't you think it would be a good idea if Jim had a blood test?' he said.

It hadn't crossed her mind. It hadn't crossed mine. You get used to something because it was presented as fact and you never question it. There was no reason to. Jim said the baby was his, Janie said it was his. No reason. God, but intelligent people can be dim.

Jim started crying again. I nearly swooned.

Oh, God. Oh, yes!

Followed so swiftly by, 'But in that case, who?'

'Well, of course,' said Laetitia. 'Of course. Yes. I'll recommend it . . .'

'No need,' said Jim. He was still holding his cup and saucer.

We all looked at him. I seemed to be standing next to Harry.

'No need,' he said. 'I only said it was me because she wanted me to. We hadn't been . . . for ages. She just didn't want it to be anyone else's.'

I can understand that, I thought.

'It?' said Laetitia.

Ben's? I thought. Eddie's?

'Well?' said Harry.

'What?' said Jim.

'So are you dropping your claim?'

Jim was crying again.

'Mrs Guest told me that she couldn't have children,' said Laetitia.

Oh. Oh, I see. Oh, poor Nora. Poor Jim.

But even so. The baby I have is not the baby you can't have.

Jim was muttering. 'Don't leave me' was all I could make out. I rather badly wanted to calm down but I couldn't.

Laetitia said she thought she ought to go, and took

Harry's card anyway. She'd call me, she said. The hearing, she imagined, would be cancelled. She'd let us know, she said. The moment she was gone I went to the freezer for a swig from the icy vodka bottle. The glass neck burned my lips. Turning round, Jim was leaving. I called him back.

'Jim?'

'Yeah?'

'What was she running away from that night, then? She told me it was you.'

'Eddie Bates. I thought he had her. That's why I didn't bother looking.'

'Oh.'

'I couldn't come back . . . I let her down.'

'Yes . . . well.'

It wasn't for me to forgive him anything. Nor him me. He just left, without looking back.

Lily came rushing in, brushing past him. They ignored each other. She wanted more chocolate biscuits. I held her tighter than I have ever held anything in my life. She said I was to let go because she wasn't a teddy bear. I gave her the packet.

'Angel?' said Harry. It was the first word he had addressed to me. 'Angel? Do you want to know?'

'I don't give a shit, actually,' I said. 'But she might, one day.'

'Don't say shit, it's rude,' said Lily. 'Who might?'

'You might,' I said.

'Might what?'

Big breath. 'You might want to know who your daddy is.'

'You're my daddy,' she said. 'Well you're not but you're not my mummy either so it doesn't matter, does it?' She ran out again.

Harry watched her go, looked at me, and shook himself down a little.

'They caught up with Bates this morning,' he said, 'at an airfield in Buckinghamshire. Seems he had a bandage round his head.'

'That was me,' I said, and burst out laughing.

'Good,' he said.

'You were there, weren't you?' I said.

'What?'

'The Pontiac.'

'I didn't have the Pontiac last night. Eddie wanted it.'

'Eddie?'

'Yes. He wanted it . . . why?'

'Oh,' I said. 'It was outside his house, with the keys in. I drove it home.'

'Oh.' He was silent a moment. 'Did you think I'd come to rescue you?'

'You didn't know I was there?'

'No,' he said. Then: 'It was all the timing, you know. We couldn't get him till he tried to leave; and we couldn't get Ben till we had him. I could have told you but I didn't know whether you . . . I didn't know what side you were on.'

'Nor did I,' I said. 'And . . . I think he killed Noor. Or maybe it was Ben.'

'Noor Abdulrachman? Why?'

'She was on the tapes Janie made.'

'The films? You've seen them?'

'I've got them.'

'God bless you,' he said. 'You have just made my life a million times easier. We thought they must have been destroyed. Have you watched them?'

'Not all. Not to my taste. Ben Cooper on the job, you know, is not . . .'

'Who with?'

He was a policeman. The human being would have just said, Ugh.

'Noor. I don't think he knew it was being filmed.'

'Excellent,' he said. 'Clever old Janie.' Then he looked up at me. 'In a manner of speaking.'

'Yes, I can imagine,' I said.

There was a pause.

'I know lots of things now that I didn't,' I said, 'before. I did not know before.'

'Yes. I'm sorry.'

He's sorry?

'Just sorry?'

'Just very sorry. Just incredibly fucking sorry. It . . . Can we talk about it? Not now, but . . .'

He wants to talk? Harry wants to talk? How are the mighty fallen.

He was waiting.

'Will you tell me everything?' I asked. 'Not that it matters. What with it all being over.'

'Will you? Will you give evidence?'

'Sure.'

'Shall we go and have some dinner? Or I'll get a take-away . . . Lily . . .'

'There's a bobby coming round to take a statement about the burglary. Ben raided the flat this morning.'

'I'll tell him you're already making a statement on a more important case.'

I shot him a look. Full circle.

'It's true,' he said.

'Yes.'

'A couple of points,' he said.

'Yes?'

'I only found out what Cooper was doing with you this morning, before I called you. I cruised his files and found out about the car, and your drink-driving charge and everything. If I'd have known earlier I would have stopped it. You're a bloody fool, but you may know that. And I didn't know that Eddie had a thing about you from before.'

'I don't blame you for any of that.'

'If you want, they'll both do the test,' he said.

Then: 'So will I.'

'You.'

Him.

'Mmm.' He could hardly speak.

Bitch! Was there nothing of mine she would leave alone?

'Fuck, Harry, when?'

'When I came home drunk and she was in my bed. I don't know what she was doing there. I was drunk enough to think it was you, come back to me, after all those years.'

Does that make it better?

No.

Yes.

Maybe.

'When?' I said.

'Around the right time.'

I went and put my head on his shoulder. 'Don't worry,' I said. 'We can talk about it.' Then I went out on to the balcony. The children were all down the other end, hooting and laughing in the evening sun.

'Did you know she wasn't Jim's?' I asked.

'What do you think? There was no reason she shouldn't be.'

Zeinab was waving.

'Change the birth certificate anyway, even if you just change it to father unknown. And, Angel . . .'

'Yes?'

'I'd like to see her.'

'Why?'

'And you.'

'What do you mean?'

He just looked.

'You only want your daughter,' I said.

'I don't only want your daughter.'

Your daughter, he said.

A silence. I shook myself.

'I can't talk tonight, Harry. I got no sleep last night. I must go to bed.'

'Oh,' he said. Then: 'Can I come too?'

Look at him, how sweet he is.

'No,' I said.

The children came running back up the balcony.

Acknowledgements

I owe thanks to Amira Ghazella, Sarah Acres, Charlotte Horton, Susan Flusfeder, Josa Young, Roger Willis, Caroline Gascoigne, Rebecca Lloyd, Derek Johns; to everybody who has ever written about belly dancing (particularly Flaubert); and to the dancers of London and Cairo.

Louisa Young, 1997